TYRANT
DIVIDING AMERICA

BY

PATRICK BRYAN TAYLOR

No part of this book may be reproduced or transmitted in any form, or by any means, electronic or mechanical, including photocopy, recording, or by any information storage and retrieval system, without the written permission of the author.

ISBN: 978-0-578-67165-9

© Patrick Bryan Taylor 2020

All Rights Reserved

DEDICATION

For every citizen of the world that believes America is not a place to be surrounded by walls, but an Idea that can bridge the divide and unite us as humankind.

ABOUT THE AUTHOR

Patrick Bryan Taylor developed a deep interest in learning about our American government and the U.S. Constitution as a young child. Thanks to some very influential social science teachers during his formative years, that interest became something of an obsession. After graduating from high school, he enlisted in the U.S. Navy, where he first served as an Electronic Warfare Technician and later as a Cryptologic Technician.

Patrick has spent several years as a volunteer in his local communities, mentoring and counseling unaccompanied homeless and at-risk youth. He also trained volunteers, led street outreach counseling teams, and served as a local community Executive Director. After leaving the Navy, he decided to work in the field of education, where he is presently exploring his passion for educating youth about the fragility of our democratic way of life. He lives in Southern California.

TABLE OF CONTENTS

CHAPTER 1

CHALLENGE OF TEACHING GOVERNMENT

"ALL OBSTRUCTIONS TO THE EXECUTION OF THE LAWS, ALL COMBINATIONS, AND ASSOCIATIONS UNDER WHATEVER PLAUSIBLE CHARACTER, WITH THE REAL DESIGN TO DIRECT, CONTROL, COUNTERACT, OR AWE THE REGULAR DELIBERATION AND ACTION OF THE CONSTITUTED AUTHORITIES, ARE DESTRUCTIVE OF THIS FUNDAMENTAL PRINCIPLE AND OF FATAL TENDENCY. THEY SERVE TO ORGANIZE FACTION, TO GIVE IT AN ARTIFICIAL AND EXTRAORDINARY FORCE–TO PUT IN THE PLACE OF THE DELEGATED WILL OF THE NATION THE WILL OF A PARTY; OFTEN A SMALL BUT ARTFUL AND ENTERPRISING MINORITY OF THE COMMUNITY; AND, ACCORDING TO THE ALTERNATE TRIUMPHS OF DIFFERENT PARTIES, TO MAKE THE PUBLIC ADMINISTRATION THE MIRROR OF THE ILL CONCERTED AND INCONGRUOUS PROJECTS OF FACTION, RATHER THAN THE ORGAN OF CONSISTENT AND WHOLESOME PLANS DIGESTED BY COMMON COUNCILS AND MODIFIED BY MUTUAL INTERESTS..."

— GEORGE WASHINGTON

Wednesday, October 7th, 2020. 6:02 AM

"Good morning, San Diego, my name is Gail Burdock and welcome to the morning edition of the National News Broadcast, bringing you the latest updates you need to know and when you need to know them. This morning, I'm just gonna get straight to business because -- well, we, unfortunately, have some important stories for you. News sources from over six counties across the nation have reported breakouts of violent civil rights riots in response to the growing concerns over the uncertainty of the upcoming presidential election.

The death toll remains at a total of two; however, the number of injured citizens continues to rise as we speak. We urge you to pay attention to your surroundings while you are out today, and remember we have a little over one month until the 2020 presidential election. Our country needs everyone's vote now more than ever before! It is up to you to change the proceedings of our society, and if you still need to register to vote, PLEASE DO IT!"

Conrad Augustus lets the broadcaster's words fade into the background of his drive. His eyes focus briefly on the Barrio Logan High School ID badge dangling from the rear-view mirror of his 14-year-old sedan. The name at the bottom of the badge belongs to him, but the young man smiling back is about ten years younger than the one he is greeted with when he looks into the vibrating rear-view mirror.

Now as a man in his mid-40's, the lines on his face sink a little deeper, the dark hair is slightly more prone to grey with intruders poking their way through, and the few extra pounds around his abdomen prove tougher than ever to get rid of.

Despite these small signs of aging, Conrad still stands tall, broad-shouldered; his body still clearly displaying the discipline he acquired in the U.S. Navy when he was younger. In the Navy, Conrad worked as a cryptologist, a fancy word for code-breaker. He appreciated his time in the Navy, and for most of his enlistment was deployed to low socio-economic environments all over the world. He began to identify with the struggle of life that comes with these third world countries.

Conrad's favorite part of the Navy was during the times he was deployed with Special Forces units, like the Navy SEALS, that placed him with the unique opportunity to interact and connect with the communities and people where he was deployed. At every location, he was able to learn from the locals and adapt to his surroundings. He spent many off-duty hours working with youth in local schools and was always impressed by how interested they were in learning about the world.

During this time of his life, Conrad became more passionate about the government and influencing youth to care more about their own government. This is the path that led him to take that picture on his I.D. badge, and you can clearly see, he was bright-eyed and ready to tackle the role of the newest and youngest U.S. Government teacher on campus.

It was with that same beginner ambition that Conrad decided to listen to the current events on his commute every morning before class to better prepare for the day ahead of him. At first, there was never much to report to his students, only the day-to-day happenings in the government that never directly affected or interested high school students.

A CAMPAIGN OF CONCERN

However, one morning that all changed, when President Donald Vil began his campaign for president a few years back. Every day, since then, he felt like he began living in a different world from the one he grew up in. Hearing the ever-declining state of the country literally every day gave Conrad a quickening sense of responsibility, both as a citizen and teacher.

It was difficult trying to get students passionate about a government while it is currently failing them. It has proven to be one of the hardest tasks he has ever been faced with -- even compared to his time in the Navy. Some days, Conrad wishes he could live without that feeling of guilt; in fact, he often catches himself dreaming about teaching math. He could fill the class days with problems and equations that have only one possible answer, instead of the ambiguity that history and civics leave room for. However, Conrad was never any good at math, and he does not have to follow that thought for very long before he gets bored with even the idea of mundane computations.

Conrad loves his students, but many of them do not understand the severity of the current state of the country. Although this is one of Conrad's biggest frustrations, he always remembers that he cannot picture himself filling any other role than that of a teacher. He is convinced to act when he hears about what is happening in this country, but like so many other Americans today, he has no clue what the right path is going forward.

IS OUR GOVERNMENT FOR EVERYONE?

As his last class of senior students began to slowly trickle into his U.S. Government class, Conrad Augustus anticipated a lively and energetic discussion. The students were passionately involved in conversations amongst one another, and Conrad felt hopeful that the same energy would be present once class started.

While he was attaining his teaching credential, Conrad had diligently taken notes on the best ways to engage students in topics, in such a way that it appealed to their interests. At the beginning of each school year, his methods proved to be successful, and seniors that were assigned to his class would brag to their friends that Mr. Augustus made their U.S. Government class interesting. However, recently it is as if there were no students left on campus who are actually invested in school enough to care who is teaching them.

Being in San Diego, Barrio Logan High School has always been attended primarily by Latinx students, most of whom have families that emigrated from Mexico over the last few generations. But this year was different; almost the entire class was native-born Latinx children, who had moved to the United States within the last several years.

Besides the obvious language barrier, most of these students refuse to identify with a government that had recently become so hostile toward people of brown skin. Ever since the newly elected government had come to power, many immigrants had fled the country or been deported. At Barrio Logan High School, this had resulted in over a 50% drop in enrollment since Conrad began teaching a decade ago, leaving him as the only U.S. Government teacher at the school.

A NEW DAY IN CLASS BEGINS

"Alright class, let's talk about the video I asked you to watch last night about the electoral process -- who has questions?"

Conrad asked his class after they began to quiet down and make their way to their seats, which were organized in a simple "U" shape in the middle of the classroom. This was an attempt to better engage his students; however, this seating chart seems only to lend itself to the opportunity for students to talk to one another from across the room.

"Oh, I have a question, Mr. Aug," said Dylan Oburr, with his hand rapidly flailing in the air, as if to mock the type of student who would actually care enough to have something meaningful to add.

Dylan is the only white student in the class, and captain of the undefeated basketball team at Barrio Logan High School, which much to Conrad's dismay qualifies him as an asset in the eyes of the administration.

"What exactly is the electoral process?" Dylan asked.

After asking the question, Dylan simultaneously let out a somewhat suppressed giggle, which was echoed by his fellow teammates and friends in the class.

"Did anyone watch the video I assigned?" asked Conrad.

Conrad intentionally chooses not to engage with Dylan's blatant mockery. However, the class stared back at him with blank faces.

"Okay, well, what about the discussion we had in class yesterday?" Conrad asked. "We spent the entire period going over the electoral process and its importance, someone has to remember."

After what seemed like an eternity, and deafening silence, another student finally spoke up.

"I have a question, Mr. Augustus," stated José.

José is a bright student who always sat in the front row, diligently taking notes. Conrad knew he could always count on José to add something meaningful to the day's discussion, even if no one else in the class participated.

"Ah, yes, thank you, José. What's your question?"

"I don't understand why people go out and vote for the president when you said there is an Electoral College who decides who wins...our vote doesn't really count, does it?"

"Well, class, your vote does actually count. I know that it may not seem that way considering what José brought up, but the electors that are appointed to the Electoral College cast their votes based on the outcome of the popular vote from the citizens of their state. So, in fact, your vote is crucial," Conrad explained as a few more hands began to rise.

As Conrad looked at his students, he saw something he had not seen from a class in years. He was not competing for their attention with their phones, laptops, passing notes, or one another. Everyone was focused on the discussion they were having and even looked interested and eager to share their opinion. The students finally began to participate in a lively debate about the election and voting process for the remainder of the class.

In the last few minutes before the bell rang as the conversation began to come to an end, Conrad noticed a raised hand in the back of the room that belonged to Miguel Ruiz -- a shy student who consistently handed in excellent assignments, but did not speak up too often in class.

"Yes, Miguel, do you have a question?" Conrad asked, gesturing to him.

"I don't know if the founders thought of this, but what if the president loses the election and refuses to give up power? Can't he just stay president since no one can tell him what to do?" asked Miguel.

Several students in the class laughed, knowing this was not a common question. No president had ever lost and refused to hand over power to a newly elected president. That is something that just does not happen in a democratic society.

"Class, this isn't funny, I think Miguel has a valid question that needs to be discussed," Conrad said. "We've never had to worry about a president refusing to give up power because we have established over the last two hundred and forty years of precedence in transferring power from one president to the next."

Conrad struggled to think about what to tell his class next. Yes, it was true that in the beginning days of the nation, there was a concern that any president who lost an election would not give up power, but those days were since behind us. In addition to precedence, some politicians would cry foul and not allow such a move and a populace that would not accept such an authoritarian power grabs to stay in office.

However, Conrad was equally aware that these were not ordinary times. Over the last several years, so many people in society had stopped being civil to one another; hate crimes were on the rise, anti-immigrant fervor was prevalent, and people could not discuss their opinions with one another without things escalating to the point of violence.

He gathered his thoughts and looked at his students then said, "Okay, class, what are your thoughts?" Raise your hand if you think that President Vil is the type of president who would refuse to transfer power if he loses the election next month?"

He began to count the number of hands that had been raised, but only scored a few before he realized, every single one was in the air.

"Alright, guys, I get the picture. Your assignment for tonight is to find out what would happen if our president refused to lose, and who'd take over? Would the military get involved? Which branch of government would ensure that he wasn't becoming a dictator?

"Jot down your thoughts on what you come up with, and we'll continue this discussion first thing tomorrow," he said as the bell rang, and the students began shuffling out to leave for the day.

After this many years of teaching, Conrad knows by now that the last class of the day is when students really start to lose focus. Although all his classes are disengaged these days, his other ones are usually slightly more concentrated on their lessons, since the last class is generally solely focused on when they get to go home. However, today, Conrad watched them leave with a sense of purpose that he had not felt in several years. Conrad felt hopeful, knowing that he broke new ground with them today.

A SERIOUS DILEMMA!

As was typical for Conrad, he would stay late to plan for the next day's lesson. Today he struggled to focus on his lesson plan; he could not help but replay the question that Miguel asked. "What if the president loses the election and refuses to give up power?" ***This was such a dark idea, one that certainly could not actually come to pass,*** or could it, he thought? Conrad ran through the list of possible events that would occur if a president refused to concede an election.

There is the Electoral College that could confirm his loss, the Legislative Branch that could remove him, a Supreme Court that could rule him illegitimate, and a population that would not accept it. And of course, there is the military, run by the Joint Chiefs of Staff that could refuse to carry out Vil's orders after the new president is sworn in. But then he began to think about the deterioration in our society ever since Vil had risen to power.

Vil had campaigned on the "Us Versus Them" platform that emanated from hatred of "others." The others, in this case, were people that had immigrated, legally or illegally, into our country, and as he claimed, took American jobs. When he first announced his candidacy, he was laughed off as a joke by prominent politicians and the media. He was considered a national joke by main-stream Americans.

However, something had apparently occurred over the previous decade that not everyone had wholly understood at the time. There was a group of Americans that became alienated by the vast influx of immigrants occurring since the beginning of the century. Some felt alienated by the changing demographics and the ever-evolving definition of civil rights, which is the direction which this country was slowly moving toward.

Donald Vil's message resonated with them; there was finally someone willing to point blame at a specific group of people as the root of all problems. Vil found a way to appeal to fears of this group through his understanding of marketing and branding. He dominated the news coverage almost 24/7 for the year leading up to that election.

When Election Day arrived, his followers showed up in droves, ready to cast their vote for their so-called "Messiah." The election was extremely close, and he barely won enough states to win the Electoral College, and although he lost the popular vote, he was elected as the president.

Over the last four years, President Vil had almost entirely halted all travel into the country by citizens from primarily Islamic populated nations, promoted white power ideology in his speeches, continually attacked the media as spouting "fake news," and even started construction on a wall across the southern border of the country, to keep Mexican immigrants out.

Hate crimes were on the rise, nationalist sentiment was in the air, and many leaders throughout the world began to publicly state that America was in an era of decline. With all the events that had occurred, Conrad started to see why his students thought the way they did about President Vil not conceding the election if he lost. He was creating a nation that was becoming increasingly isolated, something that authoritarian leaders often do to control their people. He didn't want to accept that his students might actually be onto something, but he found himself beginning to question the survival of the democratic process.

Although he didn't like the negative thoughts, he appreciated that the topic resonated with his students, and he was prepared for a stimulating discussion in tomorrow's class. Conrad knew he was too distracted to focus on lesson plans and needed to give his mind a rest. He decided it was time to leave school for the day and head home to cook dinner and get his mind off of the thoughts that kept creeping into his head.

Conrad headed out the main doors and began his trek to the staff parking lot, which was inconveniently located at the opposite end of the school from where the Social Science classrooms are located. Conrad's mind was focused on what he was planning to cook for dinner, when Bill, the quirky, high-energy physics teacher, approached him. Bill is always the type to spark up a conversation about random topics, seemingly wanting to come off as a pure intellect.

Conrad is usually self-entertained by his exciting factoids, but after the day Conrad had, all he wanted to do was go home. Knowing both of the teachers had a long walk to their cars, Conrad braced himself for what he thought was going to be something trivial, but little did he know, Bill was about to show Conrad why you should never underestimate the shy kid in the back of the classroom.

"Hey, Conrad, "Did you hear about what the President said today?"

Conrad replied, "No, Bill, I was teaching classes all day," in a sarcastic tone.

Bill, never one to recognize someone's reluctance to participate in his conversations, continued without skipping a beat.

Bill then replied, "A reporter brought up Vil's current standing in the polls by stating that he was currently down by 12 points against Joe Wilson, and asked how Vil would take it if he were to lose the election."

Joe Wilson was the come-from-behind, surprise candidate who won the democratic nomination for president after a long and bitter fight against a vast field of candidates and was vying to make President Vil a one-term president.

"How did Vil respond to the polls?" Conrad asked.

Bill responded, "Well, that's the kicker; you know how Vil thinks he's untouchable. He told the reporter, you mean lose to a weak candidate, 'Fake News,' those are fake polls; the media has always been against me. I am going to win this election, guaranteed."

As the two men approached their cars, Bill continued, "Can you believe he dared to claim he is going to win? Especially with how divisive he has been."

Conrad opened the door to his car and got in, looking up at Bill, he paused for a moment. Then replied, "Actually, Bill. I think I can."

ANOTHER OPINION

Conrad was cleaning his dishes after dinner, when his brother, Atticus, walked in. Atticus is 8 years younger than Conrad, and as of 3 months ago is also his roommate. Atticus had been stationed at the Pentagon for several years and recently promoted by the U.S. Navy to Commander. After his promotion, he was assigned back to the west coast, to San Diego, as the Executive Officer, the second in command of the U.S.S. Franklin D. Roosevelt, the newest and most state-of-the-art Arleigh-Burke Class Destroyer.

"Hey, little bro, welcome home, how's Navy life these days? Leftovers are in the microwave." Conrad said.

Atticus made a bee-line straight for the fridge, grabbed two beers, handed one to Conrad.

He took a long swig and replied, "I don't want to talk about it, but what did you cook?"

"It was that bad of a day, huh? We're having carne asada tacos," Conrad replied.

"How are the seniors this year?" Atticus asked, diverting the conversation away from him as he grabbed his food from the microwave.

"It was a pretty typical day until my last class," Conrad replied.

He then filled his brother in on the enlightening discussion his last class had about the upcoming election and the thought-provoking question that was posed by one of his students.

"So, they all believe Vil will refuse to give up power if he loses?" Atticus asked.

"Yeah, I actually asked how many of them believe that, and every single student raised their hand. It was the first time in a while that I have had a class so engaged in a topic."

Atticus replied, "Well, they may not be that far off. Today a memo was sent from the Defense Secretary that directs everyone in the armed forces to swear allegiance to President Vil and to comply with any and all future orders that come from him."

"But the oath is to the nation, not the president," Conrad stated angrily.

WHEN IS A PRESIDENT, NOT A PRESIDENT?

The next day, Conrad arrived at school, eager to discuss with his students what they had researched. Although his other classes were also on the topic of the electoral process, he seemed like a robot just going about the day until his final class as he anticipated what he hoped would be a lively discussion.

During his lunch break, he scrolled through his news alerts on his phone to find that election meddling was again back in the news, just as it had been in 2016 right before the election. He read one particular article about numerous fake social media accounts that were propagating news about the son of Joe Wilson, the Democrat Party's nominee, having a corrupt business arrangement in China, and being under investigation by the FBI.

Conrad knew that the spread of fake news was coming to its precipice during this election year, and he hoped that the people and the politicians would stand up against the range of false narratives, but he feared that it would only embolden people further into their political camps. As his final class of students filed into the room, they began telling Mr. Aug how much they had to discuss.

The bell rang, and Mr. Augustus looked around the room at all the eyes looking back at him then said, "Okay, class, I'm interested in discussing what you have learned. Who wants to start?"

Maria, a very intelligent and highly involved straight "A" student, spoke first, "It seems that if the president were to refuse to concede power, then the Electoral College would have to officially vote him out when they cast their votes, and that would be legally binding."

"Okay, but what if he refuses to acknowledge the Electoral College vote?" Miguel quipped from his corner of the room.

"It doesn't matter because the Constitution states that the Electoral College determines the outcome, not the president. So he will have to leave office when the new president is sworn in," Maria chirped back.

"What if he uses the presidency to consolidate his power and not leave office? It's not like he hasn't already spent the last four years literally doing and saying everything that we all know is the most outrageous thing a leader could do or say, and yet his base continues to worship him. If we are going to have this discussion, we can't accept that a piece of parchment is going to have any legitimacy in these polarized times," Miguel stated with evident passion.

Conrad now decided to step in, "Okay, okay, let's step back for a second and consider the possibility that the president refuses to concede. How would that guarantee that electors in the Electoral College would shift their vote from the outcome in which each of their states voted?"

Mateo, another shy student in this class, spoke up, and asked, "Well what if he can use his powers as president to deceive us into thinking that something happened like the election was hacked, and therefore the votes were illegitimately cast for Joe Wilson and not for him."

"Now that is a valid argument. What would happen if the president used his powers to just outright confuse the American people by putting disinformation into the public domain?" Conrad asked.

Miguel looked right at Mr. Aug with his hand raised, ready to answer the question as if he had been waiting for it since class the day prior. Conrad looked right at him, knowing that if he called on Miguel, he would get a strong and yet honest opinion. Conrad called on him, and that's just what he got!

In what sounded like the most confident and convincing tone of voice, Miguel responded loudly to the question, "A Civil War!"

CHAPTER 2

THE EMERGENCE OF A TYCOON

"...HOWEVER COMBINATIONS OR ASSOCIATIONS OF THE ABOVE DESCRIPTION MAY NOW AND THEN ANSWER POPULAR ENDS, THEY ARE LIKELY, IN THE COURSE OF TIME AND THINGS, TO BECOME POTENT ENGINES BY WHICH CUNNING, AMBITIOUS, AND UNPRINCIPLED MEN WILL BE ENABLED TO SUBVERT THE POWER OF THE PEOPLE AND TO USURP FOR THEMSELVES THE REINS OF GOVERNMENT, DESTROYING AFTERWARD THE VERY ENGINES WHICH HAVE LIFTED THEM TO UNJUST DOMINION."

— GEORGE WASHINGTON

Friday, October 21st, 2016. 7:00 AM

"We have breaking news this morning that brings great concern for our presidential election, coming up in just over two weeks. The intelligence community confirms evidence of Russian interference in the presidential election. We have been told that they are working hard to uncover all the specific details of the election meddling. We are not sure how this will ultimately impact the outcome of the election, but we are staying hopeful that everything will come to light, and our government officials are ensuring us that our election process remains secure."

THE HOME OF A TYCOON

Sunday, March 1st, 2015. 11:00 AM

Donald Evan Vil lives on the 71st floor of a high-rise in Manhattan, New York. As one of the most successful businessmen in the city, Vil is incredibly wealthy. True to its 18th-century French Rococo inspiration, Vil's massive home is saturated in gold and cluttered with exquisite detail. The ceilings are painted with murals that mimic the style of the Sistine Chapel, and everywhere you turn looks like the interior of an ancient European castle -- that was, of course, the goal when Vil first moved here.

Looking out from the many floor-to-ceiling windows in his home, there is a perfect view of Fifth Avenue -- precisely that of expensive high-end shops Tiffany & Co., Harry Winston, and Louis Vuitton. Vil has always been the type to surround himself with luxurious things to cover up his insecurities and give an illusion of wealth and power.

Often on Saturday mornings, Vil can be found sitting at his long marble dining table, drinking coffee, and carefully observing the bustle of the city below him. This morning, however, he is quickly pacing in front of the table, impatiently commanding staff to prepare for the arrival of his adult children.

"How long does it take to make mimosas? It's just champagne and orange juice!" Vil coldly yelled to the kitchen staff as he turned and looked out the window.

Today is supposed to be a special brunch with his four oldest children; one Vil has been planning for weeks. His youngest child and his wife are away on a ski trip in the Poconos.

"This table needs to be wiped again, and please use the right cleaner this time, this is expensive custom marble," Vil said as another staff member walked by.

None of his employees dare to make eye contact with him for too long, let alone question one of his requests.

"Your children are here, sir," said Vil's assistant as she walked past him and towards the front door.

Vil is father to five children, four of which are well established in their twenties and thirties and have families of their own. His youngest child, Brett, is only six years old and a product of his current and most recent marriage to Melanie, a famous model from Romania. Donald Vil Jr., the oldest, entered first wearing a tailored navy blue suit and shoes shiny enough to compete with the gold on the walls.

"Good morning, sir," Donald Jr. said while reaching towards his father for a firm handshake.

Donald Jr. was taught as a kid that men don't hug and dreamt of following in his father's footsteps. Like his father, Donald Jr. is a wildly successful and feared businessman on Wall Street. Next, Sophia and Olivia followed their older brother inside, with Jack close behind. All three children were engaged in conversation about the subway station nearest the building, and how the crowd of people coming up from the station below was extra aggressive that morning.

"If you had to ride the subway, you would be in a shitty mood too," Sophia said to her younger sister as her face turned towards her father and transitioned into a smile.

Like Donald Jr., Sophia grew up admiring her father's mind for business and has always strived to gain his approval.

"I don't know, maybe the subway could be fun -- I've always secretly wanted to try it," Jack said from behind his two sisters.

In response to the subway comment, everyone in the room, including their father, all turned towards Jack and gave him a look of disappointment.

"Why would you want to use the subway? I pay for the best drivers in this city for my family," Donald Vil said as the line in between his eyebrows grew stronger and more profound.

"Did you even see those people, Jack? The worst of this city ride that disgusting thing," Olivia, the youngest daughter, said, barely looking up from her Swarovski encrusted iPhone.

"That is what interests me so much, it would be a front-row seat to observe them ... like in a culture class," Jack explained as he tried to redeem himself.

Out of all Vil's children, Jack has always been the one who does not quite fit in with the rest of them. He chose to follow the path of academia instead of business and always bored by their closed-off view of the world around them and yet too entitled to understand it clearly himself.

"Ah, good, the food is ready!" Donald Vil exclaimed, looking toward the dining table, which had been precisely set by his staff in the time they had been talking. "Let's sit down; I have something important to tell you all."

The five of them gathered around the table and began to enjoy the spread set up for them, which included; eggs Benedict, bacon, fresh fruit, toast, coffee, and of course, mimosas. Although it has been months since Vil last saw his children, he got straight to the point of talking about his latest business deals. These included a couple of new high-rise buildings under construction on the other side of town and two recent big purchases of a yacht and vacation home in the Hamptons.

He also mentioned upcoming vacations in Prague and Paris. Donald Jr. and Sophia began to tell a story about a holiday on which they took their respective children together, but they were interrupted by their father, who was excited to present his big news.

"There are things in this country that really displease me," Vil began, changing his posture to a straighter position and clearing his throat.

"We are in serious trouble -- other countries are either beating us in trade or flooding our land with their people who do not belong here. Everyone seems to be fighting for THEIR rights, and forgetting that OURS is the most important."

"Just like the people on the subway," Olivia said, jokingly looking at Jack and letting out a laugh.

"I'm serious, Olivia, this is not something to joke about. And you're right, that gross subway is a prime example of how we have lost control of our country. You don't feel safe anymore," Vil replied, lightly pounding his fist on the table as he spoke.

"Go on, daddy. I want to hear what you have to say about this, I have been feeling the same way," Sophia said, giving her sister a hard look and leaning in a little closer to show her interest.

"Someone has to stop this. Someone has to bring this great country to where it used to be when it all started. So, I am going to run for President, and going to make this country GREAT AGAIN!"

Tuesday, June 16th, 2015

Donald Vil, his wife, and all five of his children are huddled in a circle backstage, behind a bright blue curtain. On the other side, hundreds of constant camera flashes are illuminating a podium, with a banner hung across that reads, "VIL 2016." The enormous blue curtain is in view in the background, with a line of evenly spaced American flags in front of it, stretching across either side of the stage.

The crowd is eagerly awaiting Vil's entrance; the entire country had been in curious disbelief ever since Vil was rumored to be interested in running in the upcoming presidential election. The possibility of New York's most notorious businessman becoming the next leader of the United States was enough to draw a giant crowd to his announcement.

"As soon as they start playing the campaign song, I will go on, and speak," Vil said to his family, who had been there to publicly support him in his campaign.

"Are you nervous?" Vil's wife, Melanie, asked.

"No, I will become our country's next president," Vil said, calmly surveying what he could see of the crowd.

"You'll be great, sir," Donald Jr. said, giving his father a pat on the shoulder just as the music began to play.

This was his cue to go on. Vil appeared on stage, and the entire crowd began to cheer and chant his name. Vil stood in front of the stage, before assuming his position at the podium, taking in the view of the large crowd cheering for him.

Suddenly, the camera flashes quickened somehow to an even faster pace, and Vil's eyes matched each one with glimmers of amazement; he loved every second of it. As the music began to fade out, Vil took his place at the head of the podium and waited for the crowd to quiet down before starting his speech.

"Wow, what a turnout," Vil said, moving his eyes across the crowd in awe. "There are thousands of you here. That is really, very nice, thank you. It is great to be in this wonderful New York City, this is beyond all of our expectations. This is the greatest turnout for any of the candidates, wouldn't you say?

"How are they going to beat terrorists if they can't even get people to show up for their campaign announcement?" Vil said, letting a chuckle out into the microphone in front of him.

The crowd broke out in laughter and cheers, which lasted for almost a minute.

Vil continued, "Our country is in grave trouble. When was the last time we had a victory and what about our current leadership, where have they been hiding? This current president is a total failure and is always on vacation playing golf. I promise you that I will put America first and will never have time for golf."

A chant broke out from a remote part of the crowd and quickly spread throughout the venue, ***"We need Vil, we need Vil, we need Vil,"*** and a sea of fists rose with arms raised, and waves crashing to the beat of each word.

"Yes, thank you," Vil continued, "people think I don't like China, no, I love them, but their leaders are much smarter than our leaders. We can't sustain ourselves with that, China kills us in trade deals, but I will beat China, Japan, and all the other big countries will have a run for their money," Vil said, raising his bushy eyebrows in a confident smirk.

"You may not believe me, but I know the smartest negotiators in the world. I know the good ones, I know the bad ones, I know the overrated ones. We got a lot of them that are overrated. They're no good, they think are, but they only get good stories in the press, since the newspapers get buffaloed. But they're not good. I know the best negotiators in the world. I'd say there's one for each country and for America, I'm that one. Believe me, folks, we'd do very well."

"We need Vil, we need Vil, we need Vil…, as the hands go up, and the waves grow more substantial in a strong current.

"Our borders are a huge problem. When Mexico sends its people, they're not sending their best. They're not sending people like you." Vil continued, pointing to a person in the crowd. "They're not sending you," Vil said, pointing his finger toward one person than another.

"They're sending people that have lots of problems, and they're bringing those problems to us. They're bringing drugs, they're bringing crime, they're rapists, however some, I assume, are good people."

Vil paused to take a sip of water before continuing with a half-smile, and then said, "I won't let other countries send these people to us anymore. I will build a great wall -- and nobody builds walls better than me, believe me. I'll build them very inexpensively. I will build a great wall on our southern border, and I'll have Mexico pay for the wall."

"We need Vil, we need Vil, we need Vil..."

"Americans will get their jobs back from immigrants; I will be the greatest jobs president that God ever created!"

"We need Vil, we need Vil, we need Vil..."

Vil continued, "These politicians cannot be trusted. They sell out to the first buyer that approaches them. I don't need anybody's money. It's nice, but I don't need anybody's money. I'm using my own money, and I'm not using the lobbyists, and I'm not using donors.

"I don't care, I'm really rich, and I'll show you that in a second. And by the way, I'm not even saying that in a braggadocious way. That's the kind of thinking you need for this country. We will be bigger, stronger, and tougher than ever before. We are going to make this country GREAT AGAIN," Vil cried, raising his hands, and pointing towards the ceiling.

A tsunami tide rose as he exited the stage, ***"we need Vil, we need Vil, we need Vil...."***

AS 2015 AND 2016 PLAYED OUT.........

A segment of society began to love the idea of a non-politician running for president, and Vil had become that figure of change in a system people had thought needed it for a while. The rise in support in the months following Vil's campaign announcement threw the entire country upside-down.

Running on a platform of intimidation and hate, Vil radically took down all of his Republican presidential candidate opponents by denigration and name-calling. It did not take long for Vil to become the only Republican candidate with the public interest; supporters were obsessed with his every move, and the opposition was outraged. Seemingly overnight, a divide emerged in the country, and more attention was on an American election than in decades before.

The Democratic presidential candidate, Samantha Allison Tan, was not only a woman but was born to a Chinese immigrant father. Her vision of American's future was quite different than Vil's and was considered a threat to Vil and his supporters. Born and raised in Long Island, New York, Tan grew up in a vastly different lifestyle than Vil and has grown to represent the people who oppose him.

Unlike any presidential candidate before, Vil has used social media as the leading platform to comment and rant, rather than about the campaign or political issues. Here he has publicly questioned many things about Tan's legitimacy as not only a candidate but as an American in general.

@realDonaldEVil -- Samantha Tan claims to be born in Long Island, but I know sources who have confirmed her birthplace as China, just like her immigrant father. Who wants a fraud as their president?

Vil's actions not only revealed a lot about his character but about that of his supporters as well. During interviews, debates, and on social media, Vil continued to use hateful and unprofessional rhetoric to the point in which many people were left wondering if he was solely trying to run on shock value, instead of answering questions and explaining a coherent policy agenda. He would resort to saying offensive remarks about the other candidates to diverge attention and dodge questions altogether.

Extremists were on his side, saying a tough revolutionary type of politician is precisely what was needed; however, a majority of Americans believed everything about the campaign was simply a joke. How could a famously harsh businessman be what the country needs? Every day leading up to the party nomination felt like another episode of an absurd drama or reality show.

It seemed like the whole nation was collectively laughing, so nobody was prepared when he actually won the Republican nomination. That is when everyone was faced with the reality that groups of people actually identified with Vil's hate speech and lambasting approach to politics.

Saturday, October 29th, 2016

The last few days before the election were muddled with tension, as both sides remained confident they would come out ahead. Both Vil and Tan confronted each other fearlessly in debates and had passionate supporters committed to showing up and casting ballots for them on Election Day. The American citizens themselves seemed equally divided among the two sides; no one knew which way the majority would ultimately lean.

That was, of course, until an old audio clip was leaked of Vil saying crude comments about women. Once the news broke, it spread like wildfire across social media where people accused Vil of being sexist and unfit to be the President of the United States. In the audio clip, Vil can be heard clearly, yet from afar as if recorded by someone without Vil's knowledge, saying, ***"I can get any bitch I want, I am rich. They love me. I just go ahead and grab them by the pussy, they won't stop me."***

His statement is followed by what sounds like a few high-fives and the sounds of other men concurring with the statement. In the past, other presidents have had massive scandals concerning infidelity, and the exploitation of young women, so people were sure this would finally bring down the giant and open people's eyes before the election.

Within just a few hours of this news breaking, however, random social media accounts that were only made the same day began to post a doctored birth certificate for Tan, claiming to prove she was born in China and not actually the child of immigrants she claimed to be. This caused people to begin attacking Tan, saying she was an immigrant herself, and not a lawful presidential candidate.

Vil began to post about this on social media since it was something he claimed before about Tan, but now there was this so-called "proof." This scandal quickly brushed Vil's leaked audio under the rug, and more and more citizens were beginning to doubt the credibility of Tan. For the remainder of the campaign, Tan was met with an onslaught of attacks from even more fake media sources, all claiming she was sending secret emails to known terrorist groups, and a multitude of other blatant lies. The media coverage was non-stop; meanwhile, Vil was consistently joining in on social media and spreading this fake news.

Vil used this as an opportunity to "gain the trust" of people, ironically making the point that other politicians, like Tan, are corrupt and only in the business for money and deception. Tan fought these accusations until the very last minute before the election, but they had caused her popularity to drop and ultimately cost her the election. Vil only won by a slight majority of votes cast, in only three competitive states. However, this minor difference in votes was just enough to change the outcome because of the Electoral College process, making Vil the president-elect.

Friday, January 5th, 2018

A year into his presidency, Vil was required to attend an international summit of nations in Moscow, Russia. It was here that he was scheduled to have his first private meeting with Russian President, Vladimir Porchensky since becoming president. Vil arrived at the Kremlin ahead of schedule, seemingly eager to meet with Porchensky. The tall building stood above Vil's head, immaculate with fine detail stretching upward to meet large multi-colored onion-shaped domes at the top.

“It’s beautiful, don’t you think, sir?” said one of Vil’s aides as they piled out of the SUV and headed towards the meeting.

“Well it’s no New York City, now is it?” Vil said, looking up at the structure one last time and distorting his face in a confused manner, “and I’ve seen it all before anyway. You do a lot of traveling when you have the life I do.”

The group was greeted by Porchensky’s secretary and a Russian interpreter, who approached Vil and his secret service cautiously.

“Good morning sir, I am so sorry, but President Porchensky is not ready yet, he just took an important call. We apologize for this inconvenience, but please have a seat in our lobby, he will be right with you,” the Russian interpreter said after the secretary spoke the words in Russian.

“Do you know who you have in your office today? This is the President of the United States and--,” the head of Vil’s secret service began to say before he was cut off.

“No, that is not necessary Porchensky is an important, busy man, we can wait,” Vil said in a friendly tone that seemed to have shocked his entire team, based on the exchange of looks they gave one another before shrugging their shoulders and following Vil deeper into the lobby.

Compared to the extravagant outside, the inside of the building was surprisingly minimal. High-quality waiting chairs lined on a lush red rug in the middle of the room and gold-framed pictures of a straight-faced Porchensky posing with different country leaders from around the world were hung on the walls. Vil took a seat next to the door of Porchensky’s office and impatiently shifted in his chair until Porchensky emerged.

"Donald, welcome to Russia," Porchensky said calmly as he halfway walked out of his office and motioned for Vil to join him inside, please, come in, I am excited to speak with you."

Vil got up and entered the office, and his security began to file in closely behind him when Porchensky held up his hand and said, "If you men do not mind, I would like for the meeting to be just us two."

"At ease, fellas, I will be just fine," Vil said to his security without even turning around to look back at them.

His security reluctantly looked at each other and shrugged, knowing if they questioned him in front of Porchensky, they would cause a big scene that may end in embarrassment for the president. Instead, they remained in the lobby and watched as the two disappeared behind the office door.

"It has been a while since I saw you," Porchensky said, curling the sides of his thin mouth into a knowing smile, "what has it been four years since you visited here last?"

"Yes, sir -- 2014," Vil replied, matching Porchensky's wicked smile with one of his own.

Four years prior, Vil had been visiting Russia for the grand opening of the Moscow location of one of his condominium properties. It was rumored in the news that while Vil was there, he desired to meet with Porchensky. However, nobody seemed to know for sure if a meeting between the two ever occurred. Back then, Vil was still solely known as a crude businessman, and no one really cared to dig deeper into his every move.

"Back then, when we came up with the plan to get me elected, I never thought it would be this successful," Vil said.

"Ah, yes, you doubted how stupid those Americans really are. I always knew we could do it, I just never knew it would be ***this*** easy. You have them hanging on every word you say."

"Where do we go from here, what is my next move?" Vil asked.

Porchensky continued, "When we sent your family to America when you were just a kid, we did not know what the plan was yet. We just knew you needed an excellent education, immense power in business, and the ability to exploit the American media and their constant obsession with celebrities.

"You did very well. All we had to do was change your name, send you over with your KGB trained parents, and no one suspected you to be Russian-born. Once we saw how you took that world by storm, it seemed like the obvious next step to get you from the business world where you helped us launder billions, to the White House where we can now finally destroy America.

"We did not know how we would sustain it, but the American people actually helped immensely. They fell for every trap, and reacted exactly how we wanted them to."

Porchensky paused and took a deep breath while looking out the window next to his desk. He continued speaking, this time using Donald's Russian-born name and holding a more serious tone as if the best part was to follow.

"The hard part is done, Dominik. You have the power, and we will make sure you keep it, no matter what. We have developed new ways of interfering with the next American election, but if that falls through, I want you to claim your loss as fake news.

"We have already been building a case against China as an enemy, and if you lose, we will blame it all on them. Now that you are our mole, it is time that we fundamentally change America.

"I want you to continue creating the divide you started so that your citizens will become even more polarized, swearing allegiance to you while others will despise you. Create such a level of distrust in the government that the entire country will break down in turmoil, the stock market will crash, and world leaders will look at America as a former world power, and America will implode into economic ruin – and maybe even chaos and anarchy. Then, Russia can finally be great again!"

CHAPTER 3

THE ELECTION PLOT THICKENS

"PARDONING THE 'BAD,' IS INJURING THE GOOD."

— BENJAMIN FRANKLIN

Monday, November 7th, 2016. 7:02 AM

"Well, good morning; this is Gail Burdock with this morning's election report. Tomorrow is the big day, and we have already seen a sizeable early voter turnout here in California and all over the country in states that allow early voting. With credible reports from the nation's intelligence agencies of election interference by the Russian's, there is no telling the outcome of the election tomorrow and what impact this election interference has caused.

I'm not sure if any of our listeners have experienced changes in their social media feeds. Over the last several weeks, my feed has been inundated with negative posts and advertisements against Democratic candidate Samantha Tan and very positive ones for Republican candidate, Donald Vil. We've reached out to Director of National Intelligence inquiring if this has anything to do with Russian meddling in our election but have not received a response."

FROM THE GOVERNOR'S OFFICE

November 18th, 2019

Governor Rosa Perez was staring at her computer screen, trying to stay awake in the late evening hours, when she heard a faint sound coming from the other side of her closed office door. As usual, she was the last one in the office and sent her secretary and staff home for the day in an attempt to focus and get ahead on her work for the week.

She was busy working on a negotiation to bring one of the largest companies in China into the California market in five different cities, a move that will lead to over 80,000 new jobs and significant economic implications in the local economies.

After taking a second to listen if there was more noise coming from the other side of her door, Governor Perez rubbed her eyes and refocused her gaze onto her own tired reflection in her now black computer screen. She decided the noise was nothing to worry about. She thought to herself, "I need to focus on making sure that this deal goes through. I can't be distracted by some noise coming from this old capital building that is overdue for repairs."

Her long brown hair, though curled and styled this morning, was tied into a messy bun on the top of her head. The dark circles and crow's feet around her brown eyes make her face appear older than the forty-nine years it had actually been alive, likely due to the long stressful hours put into her job serving the citizens of California.

"Ok, focus," she said to herself as she began to review the next section of the proposal. This was a major proposal that she and her staff had been working on all month. Her desk was covered in papers with crossed-out scribbles and highlights, a mess of jumbled thoughts she had been trying to articulate since the beginning of Vil's campaign. Like many Americans, Governor Perez was profoundly concerned and frankly, disgusted, with the actions and statements of President Vil and had been working hard to combat his message with her own politics of inclusivity.

Her vision of America was one of unity and compromise, a vision that seemed so long ago compared to the recent 'Vil'ian politics of the last few years. Governor Perez quickly became one of the loudest oppositional voices against President Vil, and the growing popularity of his agenda only meant longer work hours for Perez and the other politicians committed to creating a positive message rather than President Vil's message of hate.

After moving through her to-do list for a few more hours, Perez gathered her papers into her briefcase, shut down her computer, and headed out the door.

Looking down as she closed the door to her office, a small red envelope came into view by her feet. Inside, Perez found a simple message that read, ***"Confirmed interference by Russia in the 2020 presidential election."*** There was nothing else written on the paper; no name, no contact information, no details, nothing.

The noise she heard earlier must have been coming from whoever left this note. Certainly, no one could have made it into the building and passed the security detail.

"Hello," she called confidently into the empty lobby area, ready to confront whoever had been there on the off-chance they stuck around, but nobody answered.

On the way to her car, she could not stop thinking about what the note said, who put it there, or if it were even true. She decided her best chance of getting an answer to what this note was all about was through Janice, a contact she had at the Department of Homeland Security. If there was anyone the governor could trust to give her more information about the validity of this accusation, it was Janice.

The following morning, she made the call to Janice. Janice not only didn't have any details about Russian meddling in the upcoming 2020 election, she had not heard any intelligence reports about anything involving Russia in quite some time.

"It's as if they have gone silent," Janice told the governor.

The governor thanked Janice for information, or lack thereof, and asked her to contact her if she heard anything. She decided that it must have been some sort of prank since she was an outspoken advocate against President Vil. She then asked Janice, her inside source, to reach out to her if she heard anything involving Russia or election interference.

THE CULTIVATION OF ROSA PEREZ

Early Childhood and Youth

Rosa Perez was born on a hot late summer night in 1971 in Bakersfield, California, to Gloriana and Vincent Perez, both of whom were Mexican immigrants who had moved to the states only eleven years prior. Rosa joined the family as now the youngest and only American-born Perez; she had both an older brother and sister, who moved from Mexico with her parents.

When the Perez family immigrated to the United States, they knew very little English, and in those days, there was little help for immigrants to learn the language or find a sustainable living-wage job. They immigrated illegally, and because of their limited English, they felt most comfortable living in a community comprised of other Mexican immigrants. They ultimately settled in a low-income neighborhood in Bakersfield, where several members of their extended family had also moved to when they immigrated to the U.S.

Because of Rosa's neighborhood, Rosa and her family were surrounded by other illegal immigrants, not only in her family but around her in the community as well. She witnessed first-hand the struggle it took to raise a family in a new country full of citizens rooting against them. Perez's parents worked random odd jobs throughout her life; cleaning people's houses, being a nanny, yard-work, and several manual labor jobs. Her parents did literally anything they could do to keep a roof over their children's heads.

After paying bills and buying groceries, the family was not left with many extras, so Rosa grew accustomed to a minimal lifestyle. Most of her clothes and toys were hand-me-downs from her older siblings or donations from the small Catholic Church her family attended every Sunday.

Although many students at her school faced similar struggles, Rosa was embarrassed by how little her family had as a kid and would often imitate the actions of the Caucasian kids at her school in an attempt to befriend them. However, as she got older, around the beginning of high school, she began to better understand just how hard her parents worked and respected them for choosing to struggle for the benefit of her and her siblings. Because of this, she was inspired to work hard to make her parents proud and fulfill the life they had envisioned for her when they moved to America.

Through high school, she consistently made the honor roll and finished at the top of her class, graduating as valedictorian of her class and receiving a full-ride scholarship to UC Berkeley. While at UC Berkeley, she focused on her education and absorbed every ounce of knowledge that she could from her professors. She believed that these years were the transformative years that would set her up for success, and she didn't want to squander them away like many of her friends that constantly partied.

Although she spent most of her time in the library reading and studying, she did make a few friends at the university. One, in particular, was a girl named Maria. She, too, was of Mexican descent, but unlike Rosa, she was not born in the U.S. Her family illegally crossed the border when she was just a baby. Maria confided this family secret to Rosa after they became close friends and later dorm mates.

They grew extremely close during their undergrad years, visiting each other's families and traveling throughout California. Maria never felt scared or concerned about being out in public after her seventeenth birthday. That was due in the central part because of her almost identical looking high school best friend. As a gift to Maria, the friend handed over her driver's license to keep, especially in the event of a confrontation with the authorities.

From that day forward, Maria memorized every detail on that license so that in the event she was challenged about a detail on the license she would recite it by heart as if she was her friend. Luckily, she never had to worry about that confrontation as she seemed to have good fortune. That was until the summer before their senior year of undergrad when Rosa and Maria decided to take a trip to Las Vegas.

Maria had never left California and was slightly nervous, but the idea of enjoying a short trip to the Las Vegas strip appealed to them both. They enjoyed the nightlife, staying out most nights until the sun shone over the horizon. They returned most mornings to relax and fall asleep next to the rooftop pool at their hotel until the morning would turn to midday, and the heat would become unbearable, forcing them to return to their room until they could repeat the events.

On their final night in Las Vegas, they realized they had not yet gambled. They agreed to each spend no more than twenty dollars on the slot machines. They headed down to the casino, where they found a colorful set of slot machines and decided this is where they wanted to drop their money. They both sat down at adjacent slots, and Maria immediately put her money in and pulled the lever on her slot machine, thinking nothing of losing twenty dollars that night.

To her surprise, when the reels stopped spinning, the payout line displayed all 7's. She had won the over $92,000 payout from that machine. Maria stared at the slot machine in disbelief while Rosa began to scream in excitement for her friend. After they drew enough attention, they realized the best thing to do was cash out and leave the casino. When they got to the cashier, the teller informed them that because of the high dollar pay out, they needed to provide a social security number and identification.

Maria looked at Rosa and said, "What do we do now? I don't have a social security number."

"That's okay, we'll just use mine, and we can have the money deposited into my account, and once we get back to California, I can withdrawal it for you," Rosa assured her.

Maria agreed, and once they finished with the cashier, they decided to treat themselves to a nice four-course meal to celebrate. By the time they returned to the hotel room, they were exhausted from overeating, and they both passed out.

The next morning, they packed up and got on the I-15 interstate headed back to California, where they planned to stay in Los Angeles for a few days with another friend from the university until the end of their summer break. For both of them, the drive felt to drag on for an endless amount of time. They were surrounded by flat land on all sides with mountains in the distance, although the mountains ahead of them never seemed to get closer as they sped along the interstate.

When they got to the agriculture inspection station just east of Barstow, they were not prepared for what was in store for them. They had been told about the agriculture inspection stop from friends, but they did not expect to also encounter border patrol agents at the station as well.

When it was their turn to declare to the agent if they had any food in the car, a border patrol agent also appeared at the passenger window. He looked inquisitively at the two girls, who were now quite nervous because they had not been told that border patrol agents would also be at the agriculture stop. The border patrol agent looked at the agriculture agent and said something that neither of the girls deciphered. That's when the border patrol agent knocked on the passenger side window, where Maria sat and motioned for her to lower the window.

"Your Identification, please."

"I'm sorry, officer, we don't have any food to declare," responded Rosa from the driver's seat.

The agent raised his left hand to his sunglasses and then slowly lowered them, revealing big brown eyes that looked exhausted from the heat.

"Identification, please," he repeated.

The girls both reached for their purses and handed over their ID's to the agent. He first scanned over Rosa's driver's license before sliding it over Maria's fake ID. He then looked at Maria's ID for what felt like several minutes while glancing up to look at Maria several times. He then motioned the agriculture agent to step in front of the car.

"Ladies, I'm going to need you to pull over to the far side of the checkpoint."

Maria complied, slowly driving to the side where another agent waited. They two girls stared at each other in disbelief and confusion.

When the agent walked over with ID's in hand, he told them to step out of the car and proceed inside the small building. The agent split them up into separate rooms. Rosa spent over an hour sitting in the small room, waiting for someone to come in and explain to her why they were detained. Finally, an agent opened the door and sat down on the chair at the other side of the table from Rosa.

"Where are you and your friend coming from?" asked the new agent.

"Las Vegas."

"And what were you girls doing there?"

"Were enjoying our summer break, what is this all about, officer?"

The agent stared at Rosa for several seconds and then asked, "Did you know that your friend is illegal?"

"What are you talking about? You saw her ID, she is an American. We attend the same university."

"You can drop the act; she already confessed that her ID is faked. She has been arrested and will be deported."

Rosa didn't know how to respond, so she sat there in silence, wondering what would happen to her. Would they arrest her for knowing that her friend was here illegally? Would they even know if she knew? Would they call her family?

"It's okay, miss, we verified that you are a citizen. You are free to go," replied the agent.

"But....but how did you know that she was here illegally?" Rosa inquired.

"The officer that stopped you knows the family of the girl whose ID your friend was holding. He has been over to their house several times and knows the girl in the picture. He thought it was odd that she didn't recognize him, so when he interrogated her, he was able to get a confession. What are the odds that we catch an illegal like that?"

"So, what will happen to my friend?"

"She will be deported back to Mexico soon."

The agent opened the door and escorted Rosa out of the room. The next few hours back to Los Angeles became the longest drive of her life. She cried the entire way. She couldn't help but think about how she would explain any of this to Maria's family.

When Rosa made her way to Maria's parents' home to break the news to them about their daughter, they cried together for hours. Several months later, after being deported back to Mexico, Maria wrote to Rosa. She asked her to use the money she had won to help her parents pay off their home mortgage so they would no longer have to struggle to make ends meet. The very next day, Rosa used the casino winnings and anonymously paid off Maria's parents' mortgage.

THE DETERMINATION OF ROSA PEREZ

Law School and Career

Her experience with Maria being deported left her with the determination that her future was going to be dedicated to helping those less, fortunate. That moment in time set in motion her desire to become a lawyer, specifically an immigration lawyer. She graduated from college at the end of that school year and then went on to law school.

She graduated from law school, number one in her class, and became a powerful immigration lawyer. She became a strong advocate for immigrants, passionately winning cases, and slowly improving conditions for not only the minorities in her community but for women, the LGBTQ community, and other underrepresented communities as well.

After 20 years of dedicated, meaningful work at her law firm, in 2017, she made the decision to leave and redirect her energy towards a much more pressing issue: President Vil. After Vil took office, one of the first actions he did was to build a wall along the Mexican-American border and deport as many illegal immigrants as he could.

Perez's parents, unfortunately, were among those deported. Perez had already publicly opposed Vil's policies, but when her parents got deported, she knew it was time to really get serious. Perez recognized that California needed a strong voice to stand up in opposition to Vil's policies and represent Californian's values, so she decided to run for governor of California in early 2018.

California, the country's largest populated state, with the highest population of Latinos, is where Perez grew up, and she did not want to see Vil's influence gain any further traction than it had in other parts of the country. She felt compelled to lead the nation's most populated and wealthiest state to keep it aligned with the agenda that had made California such an economic leader through diversity and inclusion. She was elected in a landslide in 2018, after a major shift in ideology across the state in response to Vil's election.

CRITICAL INFORMATION SURFACES

October 15th, 2020

Just like the beginning of any other day, Governor Perez was up early and already at the capitol building, walking toward the enormous doors of the capitol building in Sacramento with her briefcase in tow when she noticed a man who seemed to be following behind her. Usually, she would not be so paranoid. However, as a Mexican-American woman of power, openly opposing the president's actions and conduct, she has grown skeptical of other people's intentions toward her.

She began to quicken her pace to reach the doors sooner, but something the man was holding caught her attention and made her stop dead in her tracks. It was a small red envelope, identical to the one she anonymously received a year prior. Taken aback, Perez observed as the man approached her and handed her the envelope.

"Governor Perez, there is information in there that is damaging to the president. You are the only person I trust to give this to. I've tried all my legal avenues to bring this information to light, but this president has very loyal allies, people that are devoted to him even if it puts our country in jeopardy. Please do something," the man said, cautiously looking around for anyone who might be watching the interaction.

"Who are you?" Perez asked, looking down at the envelope now in her hands and back up at the mysterious man.

"I can't say, but please, just read it, okay?" The man said, while cautiously turning and walking back toward the parking lot.

GOVERNOR PEREZ ARRIVES AT HER OFFICE

"Someone just ***gave*** this to you?" Perez's Chief of Staff, Jordan Walker, asked as he looked down at the now open letter in dismay, "what does this even mean?"

"It means the Russians have been using bots and social media to create fake accounts and news stories. They have been placing paid advertisements on social media, as well as intentionally participating in steering the election in Vil's favor, to get him re-elected," she said.

"This looks very similar to what we think happened in 2016," replied Walker.

"The Russians are conducting psychological operations on the American people," Perez said, running her thumb along the now deep-set crease between her eyebrows.

"Wow, if this is true, this is probably one of the most successful political schemes in history. I mean, just last night, I was scrolling through my social media and saw a video ad that showed the pictures of Hitler, Stalin, Fidel Castro, Che Guevara, Ho Chi Minh, Kim Jong-un, and Hugo Chavéz. Then it showed a picture of Joe Wilson, and above his picture, the words 'AMERICA, DOESN'T NEED A DICTATOR,' and then a picture of President Vil displayed with the caption, 'VOTE FOR DONALD VIL TO KEEP AMERICA GREAT!'" Walker replied.

"The level of manipulation is ridiculous. The Russians are trying to swing the election, so Vil stays in power, but why? Is Vil looking out for America's interest, or for Russia's? We need to get this information out," Perez said, shaking her head in disbelief.

Walker replied, "But this is classified information, Governor. If we leak it to the press, Vil might try and label you as a traitor for leaking classified documents, or maybe even have you arrested."

"Well, we need to at least turn this over to the FBI."

"I'm on it!" Walker said.

THREE DAYS BEFORE 2020 ELECTION

Jordan Walker was three hours into a grueling report when his office instant message board popped up with a message from Governor Perez. ***I need you in my office ASAP!*** Being that Perez and Walker have a long work history going back to their days at the law firm together, one that has merged into a good friendship throughout the years, Walker did not think too much about the message.

Perez was always calling him in for minor issues like changing the format of an official letter or to talk policy, and sometimes even just to show him a funny video she saw on the internet. So he was taken aback when he entered Perez's office and saw the defeated look on her face.

"Whoa, are you okay? What's going on?" He asked, sliding the chair opposite of hers out and taking a seat.

Perez pointed to the TV mounted on the wall beside them, "look," she said, firmly.

"What's the big deal about some guy committing suicide? It doesn't really seem like a pressing issue for a Governor," Walker replied.

"That's not just some guy...that's the one who dropped that envelope off," Perez said in a somber tone.

Walker opened his mouth to speak, but stopped himself, looking back at the TV and shaking his head before asking, "Do you think this has to do with us?"

"Of course it does, he's dead because he leaked us the information. Instead of us turning it over to the press, we turned it over to the FBI, and now they are covering it up…Jordan, I think we just guaranteed Vil's reelection."

CHAPTER 4

THE ELECTION

"FEAR IS THE FOUNDATION OF MOST GOVERNMENTS; BUT IT IS SO SORDID AND BRUTAL A PASSION, AND RENDERS MEN IN WHOSE BREASTS IT PREDOMINATES SO STUPID AND MISERABLE, THAT AMERICANS WILL NOT BE LIKELY TO APPROVE OF ANY POLITICAL INSTITUTION WHICH IS FOUNDED ON IT."

— JOHN ADAMS

Friday, October 30th, 2020. 7:00 am

"Good morning, Gail Burdock, here with your morning news report. It's been a wild month, and the election is only a few days away. The latest national poll shows President Vil losing to Joe Wilson 46 percent to 52 percent, with just 2 percent still undecided. However, in most of the swing states, the numbers are dead even, meaning this election will be all about turnout."

On to other news, "A militia group in Utah had their compound raided by the FBI yesterday. They had apparently been stockpiling weapons that they allegedly purchased from a known terrorist group with links back to Iran. When the FBI raided the compound, they uncovered detailed plans to take out the governors of several states controlled by Democrats."

Monday, November 2nd, 2020

Conrad stands at the front door of his classroom as his last period of students begin to file in--each one greeting him with a smile, and a few with a high-five. In the last month, this group of students has become Conrad's favorite. As the election continues to creep closer and closer, so does the interest of this particular group of students. Conrad finally feels like he has broken meaningful ground and can truly present the current events to them while also relating to some of the dark moments in our history in such a way that makes them passionate to continue to learn more. Once everyone arrived and found their seats, Conrad began discussing the current campaign events.

"President Vil has once again been tweeting some *interesting* things, to say the least. I thought since this is our last class before tomorrow's election, we could take a look at some of these tweets.

"Let's have a discussion together about their implications on our society," Conrad said, walking alongside the distance of the whiteboard at the front of the classroom as he spoke.

Conrad took a moment to connect the presentation he had prepared on his laptop to the projector screen in the classroom. Soon, a picture of Vil, coupled with one of his recent tweets, flashed on the screen.

@realDonaldEVil -- What a shame for the Democrats, all of the "news" anchors on their channels are whiny and keep making false claims about Russian interference in our election. FAKE NEWS!!!

"That wasn't the end of that tweet, he continued with this," Conrad stated as he clicked the button on the remote to advance to the next slide.

@realDonaldEVil -- And can someone tell that Debra Peabody that her makeup is caked on too much! There is no amount of makeup that can cover up that "lying liberal" face. When I am reelected, my people will take down your FAKE NEWS network.

After reading the tweet aloud, Conrad let out a sigh and turned to his class, "Okay, let's unpack this. What are your thoughts?"

"He wouldn't have said anything if the anchor was a guy," Camilla, a once quiet, but now very active student in the class, called out.

"It shouldn't matter how they look, he just sounds like a bully," another student said.

"Bully is a really good word to use when talking about him. It seems like he always offends rather than partake in the substance of what is actually happening. Does anyone believe that he just says outrageous things to distract the media from the REAL NEWS, like Russian meddling?" Conrad asked, using his hands to emphasize his concern.

Every student in class began to shake their heads up and down in agreement, while several spoke their agreement to the question aloud.

"My mom says that he has been playing the media for fools ever since he first declared his candidacy for president," Camilla stated.

"Your mom may be on to something," Conrad replied.

"Oh, Mr. Augustus, I registered to vote!" Miguel said excitedly.

"Me too!" Was heard in unison from several students.

"Same here!" students all around the room began sharing their new voting status.

"Wow, it seems like a lot of you did. Let's do this, raise your hand if you registered to vote, I wanna see how many of you did," Conrad said, followed by an awestruck gaze as well over half the students raised their hands.

AFTER CLASS

The final class before Election Day finally came to an end when the bell rang. It concluded what had become a lively discussion about the expectation of the character of a president and how President Vil's character compares to that expectation. The students began to pack up their belongings to leave for the day.

Most of the students left Mr. Augustus' class feeling a bit of hope that tomorrow would signify a positive change toward the future. Every student that was of age to vote was determined to vote for Joe Wilson, the Democrat Party's candidate with the best chance to make President Vil a one-term president and end the divisiveness that pervaded parts of the nation. As the students walked out of the class, Mr. Augustus reminded every student that was eligible to vote to remember to vote tomorrow. A few students told him that they had already cast an absentee ballot.

Conrad remembered that he had done that in the previous presidential election because he did not want to stand in the long lines, but this year he had become so busy with school that he had forgotten to fill out his absentee ballot and mail it in. He would have to fill it out after school and drop it off at his polling site before school tomorrow. As he walked back to his desk, he reached for his phone in his back pocket so that he could set a reminder to complete his ballot when he got home.

Conrad took a seat at his desk, reviewing his notes for tomorrow's classroom agenda when he heard a faint noise from within the classroom. He thought that every student had left for the day, but as he peered, he looked away from his notes to investigate the noise, he noticed Miguel sitting quietly at his desk.

Conrad asked himself, "How did I not notice that Miguel was still at his desk? Why is he still sitting here?"

"Miguel, is everything alright?" Conrad finally asked, breaking the long silence.

"Mr. Aug, I don't think everyone should be as hopeful and upbeat about the outcome of the election," Miguel stated.

"Oh, and why do you say that?"

"My mom says that this president is a horrible man and that he is not going to give up his power even if he loses."

"Well, I understand her concern. Vil has done some very bad things with his power over these last four years. However, that's all the more reason that there should be a strong turnout tomorrow to send the message that we deserve a better leader, one that reflects our values."

"No, I don't think you get what I am saying. If Vil wins tomorrow, then he will use that victory to consolidate his power and change our nation forever. If he loses, he will find some way to use his presidential powers to still win. I don't know what tricks he has up his sleeve, but my mother is convinced that tomorrow won't be the end of President Vil, it will be the beginning of the end of America."

"Miguel, I know that this president has done a lot of really harmful things to the immigrant communities by bringing out the worst in our nation's racist history and bringing it back to the forefront. But, I want to assure you that we do have a system set in place, that if Vil loses, he will be replaced by Mr. Wilson."

"I know you have your documents and laws that you think will save us, but my mother believes that if someone as corrupt and evil as this man could have risen to the power of the presidency in America, then no documents or laws will be able to save us from this man. Mr. Aug, we are headed toward a crisis that none of us really understand right now."

Conrad did not know how to respond and just stood in shock. Once again, Miguel gave him something dark and eerie to consider. Or would this fear of the unknown soon pass?

"Miguel, let us hope for the sake of the nation, that you are wrong."

THE MORNING OF THE ELECTION

Tuesday, November 3rd, 2020

Conrad woke up with a sense of unease. He did not get much sleep. He tossed around in bed most of the night, having nightmares about the future. He woke up several times throughout the night, his heart palpitating, and his body sweating as if he had the flu. Conrad got out of bed and walked into the kitchen to make himself some breakfast in the hopes that would give him some morning energy.

"Good morning bro," Atticus said, as Conrad slowly made his way into the kitchen. "Oh, you look like hell!"

"Yeah, I didn't sleep much. This election has me on edge. I will be so happy to have this behind us after tonight."

"I wouldn't be such an optimistic bro. I have a really bad feeling about today. Yesterday I heard some guys on base talking about how they wouldn't accept the outcome of the election if Vil isn't the winner."

"I've also overhead some very weird conversations about what people are willing to accept after today. All of this fake news that has been all over social media, even the news media, gives it enough attention that people are not sure what to decipher as truth from fiction."

"Well bro, have a good day at school, I might be home late. The commanding officer has been working us really hard lately."

"Alright, bro, don't forget to vote today. We'll have pizza and beer tonight while we watch the outcome of this crazy thing?"

"Sounds perfect," Atticus shouted back, the door slamming behind him.

Conrad ate his breakfast and then got ready for work. As he walked out of the house, he realized his ballot was still sitting on his desk in the small office he has set up in the guest room. He ran back inside and grabbed it, and then proceeded to his election site. He arrived at his local election site just as they opened for the day. There was already a long line of what Conrad guessed to be over 100 voters.

He was happy that he made the decision to cast an absentee ballot, so he didn't have to stand in that line. He barely had enough time as it was to make it to school before his first class, but if he had to wait in that line, he would undoubtedly be late. He dropped his ballot off with a poll worker, who handed him an "I Voted" sticker.

Leaving the site, Conrad felt a sense of civic pride. He had done his duty as an American. But then he began to think, "Is this all that it takes to be an American? So many millions have died so that we can have the right to vote. Is there more to be an American than just voting to have your voice heard?" Conrad knew he had to get negative thoughts out of his head if he was going to focus on lessons for his students. Just as he turned the corner, he noticed a truck driving in the opposite direction. The truck caught his attention because it had a lifted suspension, which made the cab of the truck much higher than it should.

There appeared at first glance to be a flag flying from the bed of the truck, but upon closer observation as the truck passed by Conrad, he noticed that it was a large sign that read, "Vil or War!" Conrad slumped in the seat, finally recognizing that today was not going to be an easy day.

He just had to get through it and be happy to see his students wearing their "I Voted" stickers, knowing that they had become active participants in society.

"I just need to get through today, and this nightmare will finally be over soon!" Conrad thought to himself.

ELECTION NIGHT

"How many of your students voted?" Atticus asked Conrad without breaking his glance from the TV.

The news anchor was slowly announcing the results of several of the Midwest states as the polls in most parts of the Midwest were now closed. So far, the entirety of the New England states had gone in favor of Joe Wilson, the Democratic Party candidate. Several Southern and Midwest states have swung in favor of President Vil. It was still too early to declare a winner in the major swing states of Florida, Pennsylvania, Michigan, and Wisconsin.

"You know, they say that the younger generation doesn't show up to vote, but every one of my students that is of voting age, registered within the last month and voted today!" Conrad said excitedly.

Even though the night had started off on a negative note with Vil in the lead, the two brothers were not giving up hope.

"Man, it is just so cool to see the students so excited about this. I really thought this was going to be a tough year, but these students give me hope for their generation!"

"Well, hopefully, we have more new voters now than last time around. If everyone who could vote did, I bet we never would have gotten into this mess with Vil in the first place."

Atticus nodded in agreement, and the two focused back on the words being spoken on the news.

"It's a big win for the Democrats as we can now confirm that the states of Colorado, Michigan, and Pennsylvania have all been declared for Joe Wilson. This election is going to be really close. As we believe that the entire west coast states of Washington, Oregon, California, Nevada, and even Arizona will end up in the Democrat column.

"This might very well leave the election down to the two final swing states in play: Florida and Wisconsin. For President Vil to win reelection, he will have to carry both of these states along with the states we believe will go in his direction, but if either one of these two swings states goes to Joe Wilson, then he will win the electoral college, and we will have a new president-elect."

"Yes! That's what we like to hear!" Atticus said, raising his beer to the television in celebration.

The night progressed slowly, slipping into an ebb and flow between excitement and disappointment as each state's votes were announced. Although the media already predicted the outcome of many of these states, the hope that one more would turn in favor of Joe Wilson left Conrad on edge. Maybe it was the alcohol or the pure anticipation, but when it was almost, time for the last state's vote count to be announced, time seemed to slow down. The air in the living room fell still as the news anchor began to make another announcement.

"Can you believe we are still awaiting the results of both Florida and Wisconsin this late into the evening?" the anchor asked while placing a hand to his ear to listen to the noise being spoken into his earpiece. After a short pause, he continued, "It appears that we can now announce that the state of Florida will once again go to Donald Vil. This leaves the outcome of who will be president for the next four years in the hands of the voters in the state of Wisconsin."

Conrad had been holding his bladder since he didn't want to miss hearing any returns, but now he had to rush to the bathroom. After he washed his hands, he stared up at the mirror to find a reflection of him in his dress uniform, staring back at him.

"Am I hallucinating right now?" he thought.

He splashed some water on his face and looked back into the mirror to see himself in the clothes he was presently wearing and not his uniform.

Then, Atticus yelled, "Hurry up, they are announcing Wisconsin!"

Conrad rushed back to the living room, hoping to hear some good news as the anchor began his announcement.

"We can now announce that Wisconsin will go to Joe Wilson. Although much of the nation is asleep this late hour, they will wake to a new president-elect. President Vil has been voted out of office."

Just as quickly as the news anchor finished his sentence, the brothers heard the uproar of commotion coming from the street outside their house. Preparing for the worst, the two brothers stood and moved quickly to the window above their kitchen sink, which looks out to a perfect view of their street. However, what they saw below was actually a celebration.

Fireworks began exploding, casting a strong, colorful glow onto the Barrio Logan sky. People began running up and down the street cheering, hugging each other, and blowing air horns. There was a sense of relief so strong that it was almost eerie, but the brothers clinked their bottles one last celebratory time and could not help but smile as they listened to the sounds of hope ringing through the streets.

The two brothers breathed a sigh of relief. Conrad felt that the nation would be able to heal and overcome what had been a horrendous four years under a chaotic president. Through all the loud noise outside, Conrad heard the television anchor's voice as clearly as he began to ruin what had just become a celebratory night.

"Ladies and gentlemen, I am sorry to do this, but the control room is telling me that we have to interrupt the election coverage to bring you an urgent announcement from President Vil, who is in the oval office."

CHAPTER 5

ELECTION IS COMPROMISED

"THOSE THEN, WHO RESIST A CONFIRMATION OF PUBLIC ORDER, ARE THE TRUE ARTIFICERS OF A MONARCHY—NOT THAT THIS IS THE INTENTION OF THE GENERALITY OF THEM. YET IT WOULD NOT BE DIFFICULT TO LAY THE FINGER UPON SOME OF THEIR PARTY WHO MAY JUSTLY BE SUSPECTED. WHEN A MAN UNPRINCIPLED IN PRIVATE LIFE DESPERATE IN HIS FORTUNE, BOLD IN HIS TEMPER, POSSESSED OF CONSIDERABLE TALENTS, HAVING THE ADVANTAGE OF MILITARY HABITS—DESPOTIC IN HIS ORDINARY DEMEANOR—KNOWN TO HAVE SCOFFED IN PRIVATE AT THE PRINCIPLES OF LIBERTY—WHEN SUCH A MAN IS SEEN TO MOUNT THE HOBBY HORSE OF POPULARITY—TO JOIN IN THE CRY OF DANGER TO LIBERTY—TO TAKE EVERY OPPORTUNITY OF EMBARRASSING THE GENERAL GOVERNMENT & BRINGING IT UNDER SUSPICION—TO FLATTER AND FALL IN WITH ALL THE NONSENSE OF THE ZEALOTS OF THE DAY—IT MAY JUSTLY BE SUSPECTED THAT HIS OBJECT IS TO THROW THINGS INTO CONFUSION THAT HE MAY 'RIDE THE STORM AND DIRECT THE WHIRLWIND.'"

— ALEXANDER HAMILTON

Tuesday, November 3rd, 2020

"It has been a long year, especially when it comes to the election cycle. From fake news to a global pandemic to panic on the economic front and fears of a recession to renewed fears of election meddling to chaos in the streets with demonstrations that turned violent over fears of President Vil being re-elected; we can now declare that we now have a new president-elect, Joe Wilson.

One second.........I'm being told that the president is about to make an announcement from the White House. It is probably his concession speech to Joe Wilson. Wait...Why is he giving a concession speech from the White House? Let's go live, the president is about to speak."

ELECTION MEDDLING

Statement by President Vil: "My fellow Americans, our intelligence agencies have been tracking numerous attempts by the Chinese government to meddle in our presidential election. It appears that the Chinese attempts to influence the outcome of our election have succeeded as they appear to have conspired with my opponent and the 'Dirty Dems' to try and remove me from the presidency.

"Although it appears that the fake news media has called the election in favor of my opponent, the real outcome is unclear at this time. I am contesting the results, and I demand that Joe Wilson step aside as a candidate. He cannot be trusted since he conspired with the Chinese. This is an attempted coup! We will not accept the results of this election unless my opponent concedes the election to me! He is a traitor to the American people!"

THE DENIAL

"Conrad, can you believe what he just said?" asked Atticus in disbelief.

"I don't think I can believe anything that comes out of his mouth. He lost the election, and now he is spinning this to confuse the American people," Conrad replied.

"But what if he shows proof that the Chinese meddled in the election?"

"I can't imagine him actually having any proof that would confirm his allegations. But then again, he is the master of spinning fake news into real news…well, at least for his faithful followers."

Conrad finally recognized what he had denied as a possibility all this time. This president was not going to concede power. He couldn't understand why he had not seen it sooner. His student Miguel was right after all. How could someone so young and inexperienced in life, not to mention politics, have seen something that Conrad himself missed?

As Conrad continued to come to terms with what he now accepted was a pending doomsday for democracy, he noticed the news channel on the television has just gone to live footage of Joe Wilson.

"It appears that the president is trying to deceive the American people by using the power of his office to tell a lie about me and my campaign.

"It is clear that he has lost this election and is now looking to trick the media and the American people into causing confusion and put the outcome of the election in doubt. My campaign has not been in contact with any representative of any nation for any purpose.

"Let me make this clear, what the president is doing is projecting his own illegal actions of what he did in 2016 in coordination with the Russians onto our campaign in an attempt to trick the American people. He has not one ounce of proof.

"I am calling on the leaders of our intelligence agencies to tell the truth and refute the president's claim. If you don't call out his lies, then we will be in a constitutional crisis. Furthermore, I am calling on the president to show proof of these allegations he has made against me. He knows that he has no proof. Mr. President, be an honest American and end your lies and accept your loss."

CHAOS

The following morning Conrad woke up from what he hoped had been a terrible nightmare. As he rolled out of bed, he felt a pounding migraine in the front of his head. He went to the medicine cabinet to grab his prescription migraine medication. As he pondered what happened the night before, it all came back to him in a flood.

"Did all this really happen?" he thought out loud.

As he pondered that question, he felt a sudden sickness from his stomach. He ran for the toilet just in time as he hurled up vomit from his stomach. His mind finally felt clear; he knew the coming storm was no longer at a distance; it was right on the front doorstep. He showered and got ready for work. His students were going to need his leadership.

Arriving on campus, he saw several students in groups, many in tears, while others comforted them. He walked into the administration building to do his daily check for mail in his inbox. Walking out of the mailroom, Bill, the physics teacher, tapped him on his shoulder.

"How crazy was last night? Can you believe that the president lost reelection but gave that wild speech about election meddling by the Chinese? You did watch it last night, right?" Bill asked.

"Yes, Bill, I watched it all." Conrad wasn't in the mood for small talk with Bill, so he found his way to get out of there. "It's going to be a rough day on campus, you should make sure to be a reassuring voice to your students. I've gotta run!"

Conrad proceeded to his classroom. He noticed that the campus was less busy than normal. He assumed many students had decided to skip class. As the bell rang for students to proceed to class, only a handful of the students in his first-period class showed up. The bell rang for class to begin.

"Ok class, I see that we only have a handful here today. I know that last night was pretty chaotic, but why is the class so empty?"

"Mr. Aug, you didn't hear?" asked Xiomara, the most outspoken student in his first-period class.

"Hear what?" he asked.

"After the announcement from the president last night, there was a major backlash on social media. People don't believe him. A protest march that started from a social media post is happening all over the country today. It started by some students, and you know we can make something go viral in seconds," she explained.

"Wait, so there is a protest march? When? Where?"

"It is supposed to happen at noon on the east coast. They want it to happen at the same time nationwide, so it will start at 9 a.m. here. I think it's happening downtown."

Another student in response to the protest march stated, "Yeah, Mr. Aug, I think you will see most everyone here that doesn't already know about it leave by 9. I found out about it as soon as I got to campus. The only reason I'm not already gone is that I'm waiting for my best friends' mom to pick us up and take us to it."

A loud noise buzzed from the speaker in the classroom followed by an irritated voice of the principal, "We've been informed that there is a nationwide school walkout scheduled for 9 a.m. today that will be followed by a protest march. I want to remind students that if you choose to partake in this walkout and chose to leave campus, you will be marked as absent. Teachers and staff do not attempt to prevent students from leaving; however, the administration and the district do not support this, we will not stop it."

At 9 a.m., the entire student body that remained on campus walked out. With only teachers and staff left on campus, Conrad decided to take a stroll over to see his friend Bill to apologize for being so short with him earlier.

"Knock, knock, how's it going?" Conrad asked Bill as he walked into the classroom.

"Hey Conrad, it seems like today is a great day to be a teacher. I'm actually glad that there was a walkout today, I wasn't prepared for my lecture, so I can have the rest of the morning to prepare now."

"Yeah, walking over here, I heard one of the campus supervisors mention that these protests are going on with schools all over the country," Conrad said.

"What do you think will come of it?" Bill asked.

"I'm not sure. I'm worried that things will get worse from here, though. All I know is that Vil's followers have proven themselves to be faithful to him no matter what he says and does. This could really end tragically."

"What are you saying? Do you think there will be violence?"

"I'm saying that there will eventually be violence. The extent of which and for how long, I do not know. But we are now living in our generation's test to keep our democracy."

"You really think it'll be bad, Conrad?"

"I fear that we have just opened our very own Pandora's Box."

NATIONWIDE PROTESTS

Conrad decided that he would take the rest of the day to prepare for the upcoming week's lessons while on campus. While he typed away on his laptop, he used his radio streaming app on his phone to listen to the news about the nationwide protests, which were now shutting down freeways, metropolitan areas, and causing many businesses to shut down operations for the day. As he continued to listen, he heard the reporter mention that millions of students around the nation were out in the streets demanding answers and transparency.

On the one hand, Conrad was scared and nervous about these kids because he feared potential violence. On the other hand, he was impressed and proud that these kids were using freedom of speech to their advantage. Even though most of them are too young to vote, they can voice their disapproval of the president's defiance to the outcome of the election. He wrapped up his lesson preparation in the early afternoon and decided that he would go home a little early.

On the drive home, he remembered that his refrigerator was almost empty, so he decided to make a quick stop at the grocery store down the street from the house. As he pulled into the parking lot, he noticed that it was almost full, with crowds of people pouring in and out of the store. Those leaving had their shopping carts overflowing with groceries. He decided to ask a nearby shopper that was heading toward their car why the store was so busy.

"Hey, why is the store so busy today?" Conrad asked.

"You gotta be kidding me, have you been living under a rock? This president just sent the country into a panic. People at work were talking about a constitutional crisis. My boss was telling me to be prepared for anarchy. I came from a country that has an autocratic leader. This guy is exactly the type of leader we had back home that made me bring my family here," the man replied.

"You mean, you think we might be headed for some sort of violence?" Conrad asked.

"Yeah, something like that. My boss is really smart on all that political stuff and told me to make sure that my family stocks up on food and supplies because things might get really crazy in the near future."

"Well, I've seen our country manage to get through some serious crises in the past. Remember the pandemic we just went through earlier this year?"

"How could I forget? I lost my mother to it."

"I'm so sorry for your loss."

Conrad could see the look of despair on the man's face as he assumed the man recalled the death of his mother. He decided to let the man get home to his family. He thanked him and headed into the store. It was pure chaos inside, with panicked shoppers hoarding mostly frozen food, canned goods, and toilet paper. This was not foreign to him, sadly. Only eight months earlier, he had witnessed this same type of panic shopping.

At that time, the world experienced the beginning stages of a major novel virus pandemic. The virus, which originated in China, killed thousands in one of their most populated metropolitan cities. Once it spread beyond the border of China into other nations, it spread at such a rapid rate, that the number of infected began to double almost every day.

The virus was easily spread by body contact and even through the air. This unusual virus was able to last on surfaces for several hours. As the word was spread about the high contagious nature of the virus, it was only a matter of time before panic eventually set in.

When the virus reached the shores of the United States, in all the chaos and lack of leadership from the federal government, the people went into a state of panic. All over the nation, grocery stores were ransacked by people emptying their shelves. The entire nation eventually came grinding to a halt; schools closed, restaurants shut down, the airlines stopped flying, and millions of workers lost their jobs.

Cities started putting their citizens in a period of lock-down to slow the spread of the novel virus. Eventually, several states followed suit as the number of infected grew exponentially in a short period. Finally, after several governors and other elected leaders begged for a nation-wide lock-down, President Vil issued a statement encouraging people to stay home to stop the spread of the virus, and most complied. It eventually became known as 'The Great Social Distance Pandemic,' referring to the guidance given by authorities to keep a social distance from each other to prevent the spread through human contact.

Hundreds of millions of people worldwide were infected. Over one million worldwide eventually died from the virus. Millions of Americans were infected, and over one hundred thousand died. By late summer, the virus essentially disappeared, and no more cases of infection were reported.

Conrad recalled the experience, hoping to never witness such an event ever again. Yet, here he was, witnessing the same panic he had seen earlier in the year. This time it wasn't because of a pandemic; it was because of fear of authoritarianism. Many of Conrad's neighbors fled from authoritarian nations to the United States, for a chance of a better life.

They knew first-hand what autocracy looks like, and that is why they are stocking up. Conrad decided to quickly grab a few things that weren't being fought over. He weaved in and out of the packed aisles to grab the few things he needed to get. He ended up getting only some fresh salmon, a few lemons, and green beans.

He could prepare the salmon over rice with green beans on the side for dinner. Thankfully he had a large bag of rice in his pantry at home because he saw only empty shelves where the rice would normally be located. Since everyone was stockpiling for what he could only presume they feared as the end of times, the checkout lines were all several people deep.

With only three items in his hands, he was able to check in the speed line, which he was amazed only had a few people in it. He made it out of the store in only a few minutes.

After Conrad got home, he went for a late afternoon run to clear his mind. His short one-mile run turned into a long five-mile hike as he observed panicked people everywhere on the streets and in the neighborhoods. When he got home, he showered and then prepared dinner for both him and Atticus, knowing that he would get home around his usual 7 p.m. time.

He took in the aroma of the salmon he had just prepared, which made him realize he had not eaten all day and was ready to devour his meal. He grabbed his plate and headed for the couch to sit down and eat while catching up on the latest news about the confusion over the election outcome. Just then, Atticus walked through the front door.

"Hey Conrad, did you get my text? We have to talk."

"No, I haven't looked at my phone since I got home a few hours ago. What's up?"

"We have been ordered to get underway tomorrow. With everything going on, the entire Pacific Fleet is being ordered out to sea tomorrow morning. We haven't been told specifics, we haven't even been told how long we will be gone or for what reason we are getting underway."

"Do you think this is because of the election?"

"Of course, it is! Look, I'm worried about my commanding officer. He's been sounding crazier and crazier these last few months. I'm going to go pack up some essentials and head to bed. Remember that encrypted satellite phone I gave you?"

"Yeah."

"Do you still have it?"

"It's in a drawer in my nightstand."

"Make sure you keep it on you. I have mine in my stateroom on the ship. If I hear anything about what is happening, I will call you on it."

"Okay, I will keep it near me all the time. Hey, before you pack up and go to bed, grab some dinner. I made salmon."

"Thanks, bro!"

Atticus grabbed some rice and salmon, leaving the green beans in the tray. He always hated green beans and never understood why his older brother cooked them with almost every meal. He said goodnight to Conrad and headed down the hall to his room.

CHAPTER 6

THE SPY

"SAFETY FROM EXTERNAL DANGER IS THE MOST POWERFUL DIRECTOR OF NATIONAL CONDUCT. EVEN THE ARDENT LOVE OF LIBERTY WILL, AFTER A TIME, GIVE WAY TO ITS DICTATES. THE VIOLENT DESTRUCTION OF LIFE AND PROPERTY INCIDENT TO WAR, THE CONTINUAL EFFORT AND ALARM ATTENDANT ON A STATE OF CONTINUAL DANGER WILL COMPEL NATIONS THE MOST ATTACHED TO LIBERTY TO RESORT FOR REPOSE AND SECURITY TO INSTITUTIONS WHICH HAVE A TENDENCY TO DESTROY THEIR CIVIL AND POLITICAL RIGHTS. TO BE MORE SAFE, THEY AT LENGTH BECOME WILLING TO RUN THE RISK OF BEING LESS FREE."

— ALEXANDER HAMILTON

Thursday, November 5th, 2020. 9:00 am

"Good morning, we are tracking some major, rapidly developing news. Just moments ago, Governor Perez of California issued a statement to the nation regarding the election. She made some bold allegations that she has been briefed on intelligence data that contradicts what President Vil has been telling the American people. In her statement, she claimed that the intelligence confirms election meddling in the 2020 presidential election by the Russians and NOT, I repeat, NOT by the Chinese as the president has claimed.

She went on to say that the Russian meddling was done at the orders of Russian President Vladimir Porchensky to help President Donald Vil win reelection. However, it appears that their attempt to meddle, similar to what they did in 2016, failed this time. This is a rapidly developing story, and we will bring you more as the day progresses."

ATTEMPT TO FLEE

Governer Perez' office: "Governor, Governor, we need to get you to the emergency operations center. The San Francisco Airport just went on lockdown after an apparent assassination!" exclaimed Jordan, her chief of staff, as he rushed into her office.

"What are you talking about? Why would I need to go to the emergency operations center because someone was killed at SFO?" the governor asked.

"It appears that he was scheduled for a flight to Beijing and was found with a laptop and several hard drives, but I don't have all the details yet. Once we get to the emergency operations center, we are going to patch in live and receive an update by the head of SFO security operations."

The governor, accompanied by her chief of staff and several advisors, headed down the hall toward the emergency operations center. Governor Perez overheard several of her advisors whispering about the breaking news developments. What she learned on the long walk down the hall was that the news was rapidly spreading like wildfire on social media after several accounts had posted pictures and video of the dead victim in the airport.

"Good afternoon governor, we have the head of security operations for the SFO airport on the line," stated the head of the governor's communications team.

"Thank you," the governor replied.

"Go ahead, Mr. Johnson, the governor, is here," continued the head of the communications team while handing Governor Perez an iPad with digital images of the scene.

"Hello there governor, I want to give you the latest updates we have before I brief the president and then give a press briefing later today. At approximately 2:12 pm, the victim was captured on security cameras entering a men's restroom after going through the TSA security checkpoint. At 2:16 pm, the victim was captured on security cameras departing the restroom and within seconds fell to the floor as captured by several security cameras.

"Several bystanders approached the victim, who was found unresponsive. Within a minute, airport security officials arrived on the scene. He was confirmed dead by our emergency response coordinators after they arrived on the scene. They have identified a small pinprick like hole along the backside of his neck.

"The area was immediately contained, and currently, we are questioning everyone that was in the vicinity. Additionally, we are going through all security camera footage to identify everyone that could have potentially interacted with the victim. At this point, we have identified a potential suspect, an Asian looking man seen on security footage entering the restroom moments after the victim and departing the restroom before the victim.

"The man was then seen immediately heading toward the airport exit, and we are attempting to track him from there. Now, to the victim and why this is of urgent concern since he was found carrying a Chinese passport, two laptops, and several hard drives. We contacted the FBI, and they arrived on the scene to coordinate with our team.

"However, agents from the Central Intelligence Agency showed up shortly after the FBI, and after speaking with the lead FBI agent on the scene, we were told that due to national security concerns, they were taking everything found on the victim."

"Mr. Johnson, did you get the names of the CIA agents?" asked the governor.

"We were told that we could not take down their information and that all questions we have should be referred to the FBI."

"So, you are being stopped in your investigation by the federal government?"

"It appears so. I'm sorry I have to go; I'm being told that I have to go brief the president now."

"Okay, thank you. We will have some more questions for you shortly, and I will have my chief of staff contact you," Gov. Perez replied, concluding the call.

The governor remained at her seat. Thinking to herself, "did we somehow get this wrong? Was it really the Chinese involved in our election meddling, or was it the Russians? This president has taken advantage of every opportunity to confuse the people of this nation by sending us on wild goose chases. What will happen now?"

"Governor, do you think that this could have been the Chinese, or do you think the Russians are involved in this?" her chief of staff asked.

"Of course it was the Russians! This is a ruse meant to deceive the American people, and we have to get to the bottom of it."

AN HOUR LATER

"Can you believe it, Junior? The Russians came through for me again. They must have set up one of their spies to be a patsy and take the fall for the election. They are so incredible at this spy stuff! This will help me get the credibility to claim the election meddling was from the Chinese. Everyone will believe me!" exclaimed President Vil to his son Don Jr.

"Yes, father, this is great news! You should send out a tweet so the fake news media will start talking about it.

"It will send them into a frenzy. You know they have tried everything they could to ruin your amazing reputation, and they have failed every time," Don Jr. replied.

"Let me think of a great way to tweet this to spin them up."

@realDonaldEVil -- The Chinese spy was caught fleeing the country today! He was killed while attempting to flee to China, most likely at the authorization of the Chinese government. This proves Chinese meddling. It is time for the GREAT American people to stand with their PRESIDENT and declare the election a fraud! #FourMoreYears.

"Yep, that'll do it! The press will talk about that for days. Now, once the Russians figure out that was my message to them, they will confirm it with their own announcement, and we will have this thing in the bag. I've only dreamt of this kind of power my entire life. After having control over the entire population like this, I'm not giving it up!" President Vil stated as he looked at his son with a devilish smile.

"You are so smart, father! I can't wait for you to unveil your plan to remove that blowhard of a vice president you picked with me so that we can treat this just like the family business. I can take over this gig, and we will control this country like we were meant to!" exclaimed Don Jr.

"Oh, you think that my plan was to give YOU the number two spot? Come on now, you think I would give you that power? You almost ran the family business into bankruptcy, you couldn't keep your stories straight when the press tried to take me down over this whole 2016 Russian election meddling crap.

"Now, you think I'm going to name you as my vice president? No way in hell is that going to happen! I'm going to be naming your sister Sophia to be my number two. She's so beautiful, she did so well with her businesses; the Senate will confirm her so quickly because she will be the first woman vice president, and I will be the Republicans that made it happen. We can shove it in the face of those dirty Democrats!" President Vil replied while staring at a picture of his daughter Sophia on his desk.

Don Jr. stared at his dad, coming to terms with the fact that he would never live up to his father's expectations. His sister Sophia was his father's favorite child, the one he obsessed over and always said great things about, and never gave praise to his other children.

"Okay father, as long as I can keep running the family business," Don Jr. replied as he headed for the door.

THE RUSSIAN RESPONSE

"This is breaking news, just into our news desk," started Andrew Mullen, the veteran television news anchor, "Russian President Vladimir Porchensky has just issued a statement that I will read.

"The Russian intelligence agencies confirm the death of a Chinese spy at the San Francisco Airport. Our intelligence agencies had been tracking this spy's actions in the United States of America once we became aware of his activities in the country. Our intelligence resources confirm the Chinese meddling into the U.S. election.

"Our intelligence agencies tracked the Chinese agent's activities and have identified that he used social media to sway the opinion of the American people in favor of Joe Wilson and against President Vil.

"Based on this evidence, it is the Russian Federation's assessment that the 2020 U.S. presidential election should be invalidated. That ends the statement from Russian President Porchensky. We will be bringing in some experts to make sense of all this. We will be right back."

Governor Perez couldn't believe what she was hearing. The Russians were now verifying the disinformation campaign that the president had just started pushing a few days prior. She stirred in her chair, questioning what her next steps would be. She couldn't believe that the media or the American people would just accept this statement at face value.

"They will most certainly do investigative reporting to verify President Porchensky's claim. Or would they even be able to?" she thought.

She pushed her chair away from her desk and stood up. Questions began to fill her mind, and she began to pace around her office, thinking of solutions to them. She needed to act fast to prevent the media from falling into this trap and allowing the people to be confused and questioning the validity of the election. Then she began to recognize that she couldn't go too far with her actions.

If she started pushing an anti-Vil narrative, she would be attacked by the media for being partisan. If she didn't act, she would be failing the people by allowing them to be tricked. After considering her options, she reluctantly chose to hold off on taking any action until the Chinese government had time to respond, and she could consult with her own intelligence agency contacts in the government.

THE CHINESE DENIAL

"Well, it has only been a little over an hour since we brought you the breaking news of President Porchensky's claim that they confirm a Chinese spy was working in the U.S. in an election meddling effort to sway the election in favor of Joe Wilson. I have just been handed the Chinese government's response to these allegations," Andrew Mullen stated with a tone of apprehension in his voice.

"The Chinese government denies any involvement of any form in the U.S. presidential election. It is the policy of the Chinese government to allow for free and fair elections by every democratic nation without interference by outside influences. The individual found dead at the San Francisco Airport has no connection to the Chinese government and is not a Chinese national.

"Furthermore, it is questionable why the Russian government's claim was issued so quickly after the tweet issued by the U.S. president. Our intelligence sources believe that the Russian government is deeply involved in an attempt to meddle in the U.S. presidential election in favor of their preferred candidate, President Vil. We urge the American people not to be deceived by this Cold War-style propaganda campaign.

"And there you have it, that is the statement issued by the Chinese government. I think we now have more questions than answers. Our president and the Russian president are pointing the blame at the Chinese, and the Chinese are pointing the blame at the Russians.

"I'm not sure we can make sense of this just yet," Andrew Mullen continued.

His,voice faded into the distance, drowned out by a boisterous President Vil, who had been watching the news almost daily, which was normal for him.

"HAHAHAHA! Look at that! Vladimir got the message and responded better than I could have imagined. Look at those stupid Chinese, they were too late to respond, and their message will only be seen as an attempt to deflect their election meddling back to the Russians!" Vil exclaimed.

"But the Russians were responsible for the election meddling," replied Don Jr.

"Of course they were, stupid! And you think you are capable of being my number two? Your sister has more smarts than you!" Vil vehemently replied as he gestured for his eldest son to leave the oval office.

THE GOVERNOR REACTS

"What do we do now, governor?" asked Jordan Walker after listening to the response from the Chinese government.

"Well, now the press is out there covering the Chinese response like they were involved and attempting to point the finger back at the Russians. I just read one news report that just came out saying this is all a big mess, and it only serves us right for letting Vil sweep the wave of popularity back in 2016.

"The only person we can really trust is our president to get us through these dark times," Governor Perez said, "but it is up to the American people, and their leaders to do the right thing…the constitutional thing."

"You mean that you think that Joe Wilson will become the president when this whole mess is over?" Jordan asked.

"That is what the Constitution states, and that is what the American people decided. This president can throw up all the chaff in the air he wants. He can even get help from the Russians to make this a bigger mess. But at the end of this, the American people made their decision. They want to move forward with a solid, sound, tried, and tested leader to unite us as a nation and get us out of this mess.

"We've had many trials over these last few years, but after the failure, we all witnessed by this president from this virus pandemic earlier this year, left our nation in bitter turmoil," she continued, "But we need to begin to prepare for the worst. I have a great working relationship with several governors. I am going to make some calls today to get their thoughts on this. We need to see what significant measures we can take to protect ourselves from this president."

"Wait, I followed all of that up until you said that 'we need to see what significant measures we can take to protect ourselves from this president,'" Jordan continued, "What exactly do you mean?"

"I think it is time that we begin to prepare for the worst-case scenario, Jordan."

"And by worst-case scenario, what exactly do you mean?"

"I think it's fairly obvious. I think you know it, but you don't want to say it out loud for fear that it could become a reality."

"You mean…that the president might not give up power?"

"Yes, that is exactly what I mean. Vil has tested the will of the people, he has broken so many norms, he has cost far too many lives to be lost, and now he has floated the idea that he should have won the election had it not been for this fake Chinese election meddling. I never thought in our lifetime we would see our great democracy fall apart, but I believe we might be on the verge of something that may test the will of a nation far beyond anything any of us have ever witnessed in our lifetime."

"So, what exactly do you think we can do?"

"I'm not exactly sure at this point. I need to have conversations with some of the governors and senators and assess the situation. We need to get a grasp of what they think might be on the horizon and formulate a potential contingency plan."

"Governor, you are about to give me a heart attack! This all just seems so insane! I know that this president has tested the limits of our Constitution, and he has polarized our nation in ways we haven't seen since the Civil War; but do you really believe he is capable of being able to trick the people into thinking he should remain president?

"I mean, that would require several of the electors of the Electoral College to vote differently than the outcome of their state's popular vote. That would require the people to accept that outcome. I just can't see that happening."

"In normal times, I would absolutely agree with you. I would tell you that not one American would fall for his tricks. But these are not normal times, and that man is not normal. He has found a way to trick people for years. He profited from taking advantage of the poor and disadvantaged and found his way into the most powerful position of our government by using fear to divide our nation. We have come to a point where we are so polarized, and not because we disagree, but because we are either 'all in' or 'all against' this man.

"America is better than any one of its leaders. Still, to him, it is all about his ego," the governor paused for a moment as she stared at a painting of George Washington that hung from the wall. She continued, "Our first president recognized that. One of his greatest fears was that a president could rise to power and find a way to remain there.

"He refused to run for a third term as a way of setting a precedent that the leaders are there at the will of the people and not that the people are there to serve the leaders. We have had 44 presidents that have recognized that precedent, accepted the will of the people, and left office with dignity.

"This man, I fear, will not only fail to step down but will find a way to use the tools of government to ensure he will not be removed. And I fear that the American people will not rise up against him. What I hope for is that I am completely wrong and that we will not find ourselves in a constitutional crisis!"

CHAPTER 7

PRESIDENTIAL TAKEOVER IMMINENT

"THE REPUBLICAN PRINCIPLE DEMANDS THAT THE DELIBERATE SENSE OF THE COMMUNITY SHOULD GOVERN THE CONDUCT OF THOSE TO WHOM THEY ENTRUST THE MANAGEMENT OF THEIR AFFAIRS; BUT IT DOES NOT REQUIRE AN UNQUALIFIED COMPLAISANCE TO EVERY SUDDEN BREEZE OF PASSION, OR TO EVERY TRANSIENT IMPULSE WHICH THE PEOPLE MAY RECEIVE FROM THE ARTS OF MEN, WHO FLATTER THEIR PREJUDICES TO BETRAY THEIR INTERESTS."

— ALEXANDER HAMILTON

Monday, November 9th, 2020

"Good morning, it has been less than a week since the election, and we still don't know who will be sworn in as president on January 20th, 2021. Joe Wilson has declared victory and refuted the allegations made against him. In contrast, President Vil has refused to concede the election, saying he is the duly elected leader and will remain in office. This may have to be resolved by the Supreme Court as Joe Wilson has filed an emergency hearing before the court to determine the outcome.

In other breaking news, the world was overcome this year with millions infected, and hundreds of thousands died after the outbreak of a virus now referred to as 'The Great Social Distance Pandemic.' We saw the re-emergence of the virus this weekend, with forty-seven cases reported worldwide, three right here in the United States. All three of those cases were reported in New York City. The mayor immediately placed the immediate neighborhood and the surrounding areas on lock-down in an attempt to isolate the area and prevent further spread.

The world is very familiar with the steps taken earlier in the year. It might need to prepare for another round of social distancing. The president came under criticism for the lack of a timely response and federal coordination that cost a significant amount of lives. Let's hope this is quickly isolated, and we can prevent any further spread of this virus."

COORDINATION TO DISRUPT DEMOCRACY

November 23rd, 2020

President Vil invited Senator Mitch McDaniel to his office to begin the next phase of his presidential takeover.

"Thank you for having me over Mr. President," began Senator McDaniel, the powerful long-term senator, and Republican majority leader, "It appears we have a dreadful scenario on our hands."

"Yes, Mitch, we do. We have a corrupt China that," the president paused midsentence.

"Mr. President is everything okay?" asked Senator McDaniel.

"That's it! I'm going to call them 'Corrupt China!' That will definitely be a catchy phrase. Let me tweet that out real quick," replied President Vil as he reached for his cell phone from the inside pocket of his blazer.

"That's great, Mr. President! I know you have a great understanding of marketing from your previous career. I'm sure that will send the media into a frenzy. But I came here to discuss the current crisis that you have created."

"And what crisis is that?"

"The crisis when you decided to declare victory in the election even though that was not the election outcome. We now have a major crisis on our hands. Our citizens have been rioting in the streets for weeks now, and the media can't locate any proof you claim regarding Chinese election meddling. The far-right groups are talking about 'taking out' the rioters."

"I'm not sure I see the problem here," replied President Vil, with an evil smirk slowly growing on his face.

"The problem is that I have to give answers to the American people while trying to hold back a very upset group of Senate Republicans that are telling me that they won't go along with this charade you are playing."

"Well, you can just tell them that they can rest easy because I will not be giving up the presidency. The people rode the wave each time I created havoc. What happened? Each time, things settled down, and you found out what I was telling you, idiots, for years. American's aren't as swayed by individual actions like you thought. Once push comes to shove, Republicans vote red, and Democrats vote blue. What is that 'saying' you keep repeating?"

"Democrats fall in love, and Republicans fall in line."

"Yes, that's the one. That's how I ended up here. Those dirty Democrats picked that horribly unpopular Samantha Tan and the Democrats didn't fall in love, so you ended up with me! And I don't lose, so I'm not going anywhere!"

Mitch laughingly asked, "How are you going to pull that one off?"

"Well, Mitch, you are going to walk out in front of the cameras and tell the world that 'My Republican Party' concurs with the assessment of the executive branch and that you look forward to Joe Wilson conceding to me."

"Well, you sure are one confident SOB to think that I am just going to walk out there and convince the media of this."

"You don't have to; we just need to float this concept. Look, Joe Wilson is a coward, and he will back down once the media is all over him. He can't handle the pressure. I'll give it a week at most until he concedes."

As the senator was about to respond, several senior staff members of President Vil walked into the oval office. One approached the president and whispered in his ear. The senator, sitting on the couch in the middle of the oval office, waited patiently while the senior staff member finished what he was telling the president.

"Thank you so much for that great news!" exclaimed President Vil. A huge grin appeared on his face as he swiveled in his chair to face Senator McDaniel. "Well, Mitch, it looks like you won't get a lot of push back from my Republicans anymore. I was just told that Joe Wilson tested positive for that new virus that we don't have a vaccine for yet. You know the one that the 'corrupt Chinese' spread all over the world this year. He will probably be dead in a few days. You will go back to the Republicans and tell them that they will tow the party line, every single one of them!"

IN NEED OF LEADERSHIP

December 1st, 2020

The Speaker of the House sat at her desk, mulling over the possibilities of what is to come. President Vil had just been defeated in his reelection bid but claimed it to be invalid because of election meddling by the Chinese. Joe Wilson won the electoral vote and denied the allegations made against him by the president.

Neither the Russians nor the Chinese could be trusted. The intelligence community was not providing any answers. The public was outraged, almost half believing the president to be right and the other half ready to have Joe Wilson become president.

The nation was as polarized as has ever been. She grabbed her secure cell phone and placed a call to her home state governor, a trusted friend, and colleague, someone she had known for fifteen years. Governor Rosa Perez looked down at her cell phone, wondering why the Speaker of the House was calling her.

"Hello, madam speaker. It is quite a surprise to get a call from you. How have you been?"

"Hello Rosa, personally, I am doing great. I got to spend time with my grandkids over the weekend, and my husband took me out for an amazing dinner for my birthday last night. But look, that's not why I am calling, and I'm sure you know that. I just got off the phone with president-elect Joe Wilson's Chief of Staff, and he is not doing well. The virus is taking a toll on him, and the doctors are giving him a slim chance for recovery. The country is in turmoil and needs a leader to get us out of this nightmare."

"Oh, no, that is terrible news. What will happen if Joe doesn't make it through this?"

"Well, it would mean that his vice presidential pick would be sworn in as president. But with all of this confusion after Vil threw out wild accusations, I'm not sure what is going to happen. Several electors have now publicly stated that they will defy their state's popular vote outcome to vote in favor of Vil. This will put the entire integrity of the electoral process in jeopardy. I am not sure what the future holds for the survival of our democracy."

"What is it that you want from me, madam speaker?"

“I’m glad you asked. What I am about to tell you is classified. I need you to understand that once you hear this, then you will be the only person who can get this ship back on course. You are the only person outside of Washington D.C. that I trust to take action independently and not make this a political battle, but one of democratic survival.”

“Okay, you’ve got my attention,” Rosa replied.

“I just had a briefing from the directors of both the CIA and the FBI yesterday. This was an unscheduled briefing and caught me quite off guard when they showed up in my office unannounced. They expressed urgency and discretion, so I decided to hear them out. They informed me that they had multiple intelligence sources and communications intelligence from NSA phone surveillance that corroborates what we have feared all this time.

“They showed me multiple intelligence documents from these sources that confirm the president is indeed a mole for the Russian government and that he is working on behalf of Vladimir Porchensky. The Russians cooperated with Vil and meddled in our election in both 2016 and 2020 to ensure his victory to become, and now remain, as president and destroy our nation’s government from within.

“They even came up with a catchy phrase to convince people that he was on their side. Remember that ‘drain the swamp’ catchphrase? Well, that was something they came up with to drain our government of the defenses to sustain our democratic way of life.”

“If they knew this, then why didn’t they say anything until now?”

“I pressed them on that. The intelligence agencies believed that because they are part of the executive branch, their internal agency memos require them to omit anything negative about the president.”

"So, they just sat on this stuff?" Rosa replied in amazement.

"They believed that democracy would find a way of correcting itself somehow and that there wouldn't be enough actual destruction that would occur. They thought they could instill countermeasures to slow or stop his impact on our government and our society."

"Well, their lack of patriotism has cost us a lot, including more lives, than we can bear to admit."

"Yes, and they know that now. But what I'm most concerned about is the final thing the agencies told me about Vil's actions."

"Which is?" Rosa asked.

"Vil is planning to use Joe's failing health to declare him unfit to become president. He is already using his team to work with several electors to switch their votes to him to ensure he will remain president. This will invalidate the election, our democratic way of life, and turn what have already been a few weeks of post-election chaos into several weeks or possibly months of major violence. It's very sad, but these are the times we find ourselves in."

"So what is it that you want me to do?"

"You and the other governors need to begin talking about the public response to Vil if Joe doesn't pull through. The Republicans already control the Senate, and the Democrats lost control of the House in this election. Our ability to slow things down or to fight this will cease on January 2nd once control of both chambers is in the hands of Republicans. This will take a concerted effort on behalf of the states and the people to the right this wrong and retain our democracy."

"You know I will do whatever I can to make sure that we don't go down the path Vil wants. That will be the end of our democratic way of life. I will start making calls immediately." Rosa said.

Governor Perez began reconnecting with her network of Democratic governors, whom she had a great relationship with, to develop a plan to respond in the now likely event that Joe Wilson succumbs to the virus, and President Vil uses the opportunity to build support to remain in power.

After her sixth call to a governor that day, Jordan Walker rushed into her office to show her the breaking news alert on his phone. As he turned the screen in her direction, he did everything he could to hold back tears. She almost couldn't read the screen because Jordan's hand was shaking. It read: **Joe Wilson DEAD!** Presidential confusion is now American CHAOS!

FUTURE IN DISARRAY

December 4th, 2020

Andrew Mullen, the respected news anchor, took his seat at the desk finishing his preparations before going on air to report his daily newscast. The once energetic broadcast journalist now looked sleep-deprived. Weeks of reporting on the president's refusal to concede the election, the turmoil and unrest after the election, the reemergence of the still incurable virus, and now the death of the president-elect, had taken a toll on him.

His concern was now apparent every day he went on television. He heard the countdown in his earpiece as he saw the light on the camera turn green. He took a deep breath and focused on the camera.

"Good evening America. Tonight, we bring you continuing coverage of the nation-wide protests, many of which have turned to riots. Reports of looting and violence in several of our most populated cities have left some to start fleeing for safer locations. The mayor of New York City has now ordered the entire city to adhere to a sunset curfew for the next thirty days, which begins tonight. Several other mayors are also considering similar actions.

"Meanwhile, the virus that swept the world last spring returned this fall, already claiming the life of our president-elect. There are already over 12,400 cases in the country, with 322 deaths. This has the potential to lead to more state by state lockdowns and eventually nation-wide lockdown to prevent the spread of the virus. With so many unknowns, mayors and governors around the nation may still be able to slow the spread of the virus while simultaneously controlling the rioting and looting by issuing lockdown orders."

A DATE THAT WILL AGAIN LIVE IN INFAMY

December 7th, 2020

President Vil, in his normal routine, was doing what he does every morning sending out tweets. He sat on the couch in the personal residence in the White House, watching his favorite news channel tweeting controversial statements and re-tweeting far-right talking points. Today, he felt, was going to be a great day. He had consolidated support from the entire Republican Party. His favorite news channel was in full force, every hour, telling viewers that the entire nation should rally around the president in these uncertain times.

The Democratic Party doesn't seem to have any specific leaders, and the vice president-elect was not providing leadership. He had a 5-4 conservative-leaning Supreme Court in his favor, so even though the election case was going forward, he felt confident the outcome would be in his favor.

His daughter Sophia came walking through the personal residence entrance of the White House with her husband in tow. It was time for their morning strategy session. They usually discuss the hot topics of the day and how to counter them with their own talking points. Often they found that the best way to counter any negative news was to leak a story to the media that was even more controversial than the current news coverage to keep President Vil on the news all day long.

One of their best strategies, one that helped Vil build his brand, was the idea that news is news, no matter if it is negative or not. For over forty years, Vil was on television and print media, usually for controversial things, making him a household name.

As Sophia Kaiser entered the residence, she headed for the kitchen. Her husband, meanwhile, made a beeline directly for the corner chair in the living room. Sophia's husband is a shy character, extremely anti-social. Although he lacks social skills, he is very astute with leveraging the press and social media to his father-in-law's advantage.

"Good morning, father," said Sophia as she reached for some bottled water from the refrigerator.

"Good morning, honey. Today is going to be a busy day for you."

"Oh, and why is that?" she asked.

"Today is the day the Supreme Court should make their decision that I have been legally re-elected as president. Then I will have my vice president resign and nominate you as my vice president."

"Oh, daddy, I can't wait! My husband has been working on a rough draft of your speech to give to the people after we hear from the court."

"That's great! I need to sound convincing and powerful. I need to put fear in the hearts of those who continue to challenge my claim that I remain president. This will be one of my greatest speeches!"

Sophia heard a noise coming from the kitchen counter. She walked over to counter, and as she approached it, she noticed the noise was coming from her purse. Her phone was vibrating. She reached for her phone and noticed the call was from a blocked number but proceeded to answer it.

"Hello… You've got to be kidding me! … Are you sure? … Okay, thank you, I will let my father know."

Sophia put her phone back on the kitchen counter.

"Who was that?" asked Vil as he rose cautiously from the couch.

"That was an aide to the Chief Justice. The court is not going to rule in your favor. They were deeply divided, but the Chief Justice feels that he would be upending the Constitution if he voted to keep you in power."

"That SOB."

"Keep calm, father. Have you taken your blood pressure medication this morning?"

"Yes, I did. Don't try and cut me off, you know I don't like that."

"I'm sorry, you're right; I didn't mean to be disrespectful to your father."

"Didn't I teach you never to apologize? We Vil's are NEVER wrong, so we NEVER apologize, and we NEVER admit failure!"

"You're right as always father," Sophia acquiesced, "Now, let's figure out a way to spin this Supreme Court issue back in our favor."

“I’ve already figured it out,” replied Sophia’s husband, “All we have to do is craft up a speech where,” pausing to look at President Vil, “you declare that due to the Chinese election meddling and the death of your opponent, you are the duly elected president and will remain in power. Then you will claim that due to the rioting and ongoing health pandemic and you must declare martial law throughout the nation.

“You will use the military to put an end to the riots and get everyone back into their homes. Showing this decisive leadership will force the Chief Justice to rethink his vote against you. It will weigh heavily on the shoulders of the electors that have already been signaling their potential support to vote for you next week.”

“You are brilliant! My daughter was so smart to marry you. You always come up with these brilliant plans that get me out of the precarious situations I end up in.”

“Well, when you told us of your plans a few years ago, we knew we wanted to be part of them. With all the help we have provided you in doing the back-channeling with Russia, all we want is for you to name Sophia as your vice president after the dust settles. The Senate will easily confirm her, she has built such a great working relationship with most of the Republican members, and they won’t defy you. Besides, your current vice president is a bumbling fool.”

“Yes, everything is working out, even better than I planned. Okay, now get to work, you two. I need a speech to give tonight…during prime-time television hours…so I can reach the widest possible audience. You’d better make this one of my greatest speeches ever! The American people need to remember this day!”

CHAPTER 8

BACKLASH

"THOSE WHO WOULD GIVE UP ESSENTIAL LIBERTY TO PURCHASE A LITTLE TEMPORARY SAFETY DESERVE NEITHER LIBERTY NOR SAFETY."

— BENJAMIN FRANKLIN

Tuesday, December 8th, 2020

"Gail Burdock, here with this morning's news brief. Last night's announcement by the president has many Americans concerned that he is using the death of his opponent, the pandemic, and the nationwide riots, to garner support from his party and consolidate powers to the presidency. His statement was unprecedented and audacious, to say the least. Some politicians have been quietly saying that it may not have been meant for the American people as much as it was for the electors. They meet next Monday to decide who our president will be for the next four years.

By giving the appearance of bold and decisive leadership in these very troubling times, he may be able to sway some of the electors to defy what has been a tradition and instead vote for him. This could lead to President Vil remaining in office for another four years. For those of you that did not hear the speech last night, we will break down the components of his plan for martial law.

Starting Friday, at sunset, there will be a nationwide curfew in effect until further notice. What does this mean? Everyone will be required to remain in their homes until further notice, essentially like the self-quarantine we all remember from earlier this year. You will be permitted to leave your residence only to conduct basic chores deemed essential between sunrise and sunset only.

These essential chores include grocery shopping, restaurant pick-up, filling up on gas, important banking, and some construction and home improvement.

"If you are employed in those businesses, you will most likely continue to work at your place of employment. For the rest of us, we will have to work from home, if that option is available. Remember, when you do go out, keep a social distance of six feet or greater to prevent the spread of the virus and be back in your residence by sunset each night.

Now, to the final issue from last night's address by the president. He is ordering the military to enforce this nationwide curfew. He has not gained the support of both branches of Congress, and he will need both branches to sign off on this to use the military in such a manner. This is entirely feasible, however, highly unusual."

THE DEFENSE SECRETARY IS UPSET

Wednesday, December 9th, 2020

It had been a hectic thirty-six hours for the Defense Secretary and the Joint Chiefs of Staff. They were all caught off guard by the surprise announcement from the president. The secretary spent all day after the announcement attempting to reach the president to speak with him about the legality of using the military as a law enforcement mechanism to impose the curfew.

He spent several hours working with the Joint Chiefs to determine the legality and establish how such a plan would be enacted. After several meetings amongst the group, in consultation with their military and constitutional legal team, they concluded that they would be enacting something almost unprecedented and only legal if Congress passed a law so that it could be implemented.

They were hindered by a lack of communication between the White House and the Pentagon. The Secretary's calls to the president went unanswered and were not returned. He decided that the best way to get the answers he needed was to go directly to the White House. He brought the entire Joint Chiefs with him so everyone would receive the same information directly from the president.

The sense of urgency to speak with the president was apparent, as the Defense Secretary walked through the halls of the White House. Normally, he would be stopped several times in the hall by staffers attempting to garner a few minutes of his time to talk policy. He was always one to give a few moments of his time, especially if it was to discuss issues about the military.

Today was different, he was irritated, and it was evident on his face and in his walk. No one was willing to approach him today. Everyone seemed to know why he and the Joint Chiefs were there, and no one wanted to get on his bad side. When he got to the door leading to the Oval Office, the president's administrative secretary stood up to greet him and inform the president that he had company.

However, the Defense Secretary and the Joint Chiefs breezed right passed Vil's secretary and walked right into the Oval Office, where the president and his daughter Sophia were engaged in conversation.

"Good morning Mr. President. We would like a moment of your time if you are available," the Defense Secretary stated.

"We are in the middle of something, is this urgent?" asked Sophia.

The Secretary took a long deep breath and then replied, "Yes, this is a matter of national security, so we need to speak with the president…alone."

"No, she will stay. My daughter is a part of my administration now, and I granted her all the necessary clearances."

"Ok, Mr. President, then here goes. We were caught off guard by your announcement on Monday. There has been no plan developed for a military occupation of the country. We cannot develop and implement a plan of this size, nor can we conduct a troop movement necessary to enforce this curfew in the time frame you are asking. Not to mention the legal issues we have to get around!"

"Calm down, there is nothing to worry about. My daughter's husband has already been developing the plans, and he will bring them to you when they are complete."

"This is something that takes months to develop with an entire staff working on it; there is no way your son-in-law can come up with something in such a short time."

"Well, I was just with him, and he has the plan almost entirely complete," replied Sophia.

"See that? He's a miracle worker. Now, as for the legality of all this, I'm not worried about that at all. The Senate is in my hands, and they do whatever I tell them to do."

"But you will also need the House to pass any legislation to allow the military to be used as a police force."

"You think I'm worried about passing some law? I'm not going through Congress for this. I am the President of the United States, and I will take whatever measures necessary to protect my people. If I have to go around Congress, then I will!"

"Mr. President, with all due respect, what you are talking about doing is completely illegal, not to mention unethical. They can impeach you for this."\

"Of course…impeachment, the Dems tried that before. Remember how that turned out? The Senate laughed off the attempt to remove me after those 'dirty Dems' impeached me. The Senate is the only chamber I would have to worry about…and they are in lockstep with me all the way."

"Then I can't go along with you on this. When you asked me to serve as your Defense Secretary, I did so out of a sense of duty to the Constitution and the country. This is entirely unconstitutional, and as such, I cannot justify doing this."

"Then your services are no longer needed," retorted Sophia.

"If you aren't going to carry out my orders, then I don't want you working for me anymore," replied Vil.

"Do you realize what you are doing? Have you lost your mind? The moment that Congress finds out that you fired me, there will be investigation after investigation after lawsuit after lawsuit. You will never ever be able to implement this."

"You keep thinking that I care about them. I am the head of the executive branch. That means this is MY country! I run this show!"

The Defense Secretary stood there in shock after hearing the words the president just spoke. He no longer recognized the man that stood in front of him. He had known the president for many years, since he was in private business, long before he ran for president.

He always thought he was a sensible person who would listen to well-reasoned advice. This was a different man that stood in front of him now. The only thing he could do is stand on principle and resign.

"Very well, you will have my letter of resignation today," stated the Defense Secretary, as he turned and left the room.

Turning to look at all the Joint Chiefs contingent, Sophia asked, "And what about the rest of you…will you follow the president's orders?"

The Chairman of the Joint Chiefs responded, "Ma'am, this was my greatest fear. That somehow, the president was considering an illegal and unconstitutional act. I cannot carry out these orders. You will have my resignation as well within the hour."

"Very well, and the rest of you?" replied Sophia.

The remaining Joint Chiefs looked at each other, seemingly as though they knew what the others were thinking. Then they simply turned and followed the Chairman out without making eye contact with the president or his daughter.

"That's okay, Vil said. I will take direct control of the military then my orders can be carried out. Honey, send your husband to the Pentagon.

He will be my liaison to carry out my orders from here on out. Have him craft up one of his amazing press releases where he will inform the public that the secretary and the Joint Chiefs were no longer able to perform their jobs in a manner to my satisfaction, and therefore I asked them to resign. Oh, and make sure he adds that I will now be in direct control of the armed forces."

A NATION DIVIDED

Monday, December 14th, 2020

"Would you look at that? My favorite news channel is showing that the American people support what I'm doing. In fact, they support me remaining in office another term. In fact, I think those are the highest poll numbers I have had my entire presidency; 60% of the people support me!" shouted a jubilant Donald Vil.

"Yes, father, your favorite news channel has always been more generous to you, and you have rewarded them greatly with several one-on-one interviews over the rest of the media. But I should let you know that even though what you are looking at shows more positive numbers, the overall average actually shows the nation quite split.

"Actually, it seems like they are split dead even between their support for you at 45% while 45% are against you, and 10% are unsure whether you are doing the right thing or not," a realistic Sophia replied.

"Oh, that's just fake news! What have I told you about watching those other media outlets? All they do is spew hate and talk bad about me to increase their own ratings! They make that stuff up on the fly!" exclaimed Vil.

"Yes, father, I understand that it's fake news to you…"

"And what did I tell you about fake news?"

"It's all fake news unless it's something positive about you."

"Exactly, and I call them out on it. The media will eventually learn that I reward them when they say good things about me. But when they say something negative, then I call them fake news. Look, the people like a show, and I have been putting one on for them for over four years now. They love that I've turned the presidency into a damn good reality show."

"I just think we should thread this needle ever so slightly until we get through today. After the electors cast their ballots, you will officially remain as president." Sophia said.

"And then I can finally name you as my vice president."

"I spoke with Mitch McDaniel late last night. He says that you should have enough electors to secure your victory. He believes you may even get more than the 270 you need. I guess that speech you gave last week was the right move." Sophia said.

"Of course, it was! I always make the right moves."

The father-daughter duo spent the rest of the day scheming up their plans for domination over the democratic system of government, while the electors each met in their respective states to cast their ballots. Vil, always one to be watching his favorite news channel, looked up every time the ballot tally was read off for each state. The excitement of this event kept him on edge.

He loved the drama that went along with every facet of his life. He built an entire career around drama, and now he was in the most powerful position in the world because he knew that the American people were drawn to drama. The results kept coming in, with several electors switching their votes just as they had hoped. As the day progressed, Vil no longer felt any uncertainty about his chances. He knew that enough electors had switched their vote and cast it for him.

He decided that it was time to celebrate, even though he wasn't quite over the threshold yet. He had his administrative secretary call to the kitchen to make him his favorite four-cheese mac and cheese meal. While he devoured his favorite dish, Sophia left the Oval Office to take a call. When she returned, the once jovial appearance she had on her face was replaced with that of anguish.

"What's wrong, honey?" asked Vil.

"I just got off the phone with my husband at the Pentagon. It seems that our intelligence community is tracking a lot of 'chatter' between several domestic militia groups, gangs, and other extremists. They are coordinating a response to today's outcome if it goes in your favor."

"You mean when it goes in my favor?"

"Yes, father. We may have an outbreak of domestic terror on our hands."

"Well, did this 'chatter' give us any details as to a location?"

"I think this might be something we will have to battle on several fronts."

"Well, I guess it might be time to consolidate more powers into the executive branch so that I can crush any opposition to me."

Sophia looked up at the television, which was now flashing a breaking news alert across the bottom of the screen. As she read the breaking news alert, she forgot about the conversation she had been having with her father. Her look of anguish quickly vanished as her grin grew wide across her face.

"Congratulations, Mr. President! You have four more years to run this country!" she exclaimed.

"Who said it will ONLY be four more years? I think it's time to make a call to Vlad," Vil replied.

IT WAS ALWAYS THE RUSSIANS

December 14th, 2020

President Vil spent over fifteen minutes pacing back and forth, waiting for his call to get patched through to Russian President Vladimir Porchensky. He has always been the subordinate one in this relationship. It was hard for him to contain his excitement to tell Vladimir that they could finally move to the next phase of their plan.

"Ok, Mr. President, go ahead, President Porchensky is on the line," said the operator.

"Vladimir, are you there?" asked Vil.

"Yes, my Dominik, I am here. Do you know how late it is?" asked Vladimir.

"It's at 6 p.m. here."

"Yes, Dominik, it is 6 p.m. in Washington, which means that it's 1 a.m. here!" exclaimed an irritated Vladimir.

"I'm so sorry Vlad, I didn't realize how late it was."

"Don't call me Vlad. My name is Vladimir or President Porchensky."

"Yes, Vladimir, accept my apologies."

"What do you want?"

"I have great news! Its official, the electors, have made me president for another term!" exclaimed Vil.

"That's great, but I already knew that."

"How did you know? It was just announced."

"We Russians have our ways. We didn't have to twist too many arms."

"Remind me never to get on your bad side."

"Then, you need to enact the next stage of our plan."

"Well, I wanted to let you know that I have made one addition to that plan."

"Which is?"

"I will be replacing my incompetent vice president with my daughter Sophia."

"And why would you do that? We helped you pick your vice president specifically because he is incompetent. This way, if you were ever impeached…and you were…the Republican senators would never vote to convict you because they would be left with a fool running the country."

"Yes, I understand that. But here is how I see it. They don't realize how this whole democracy thing really is so simple to work around. I will soon consolidate power and have total control over the country, remaining in power for the rest of my life.

"But, I don't want to leave my successor to chance. My daughter Sophia is a true charmer and highly intelligent. I taught her very well, and she is my most precious child. If I name her as my number two, then she will become president if something were to happen to me. She is not even forty years old yet, so she could possibly reign for fifty years. Once we finish 'draining the swamp,' then there will be no way for this country to function without 'Vil'ian leadership!"

"Yes, yes, Dominik! I like this idea. It looks like I may have underestimated you. Once you have consolidated power under your leadership, then we can finally dismantle America's economic and military strength. And now that China is in great economic and political turmoil, Russia will emerge as the great dominating force in the world. I look forward so much to visiting America. You have such beautiful countryside there, warm beaches, and Disney World.

"What is it that they call it 'the most magical place on earth'?" My children have always wanted to visit that place. When I come to America, we will perhaps visit several places, so I can allow my children to have a real vacation instead of our normal ski trip."

"We have so many beautiful places here, and some of the most gorgeous beaches! You can stay at any of my resorts around the country. They have the best golf courses in the world! We will give you a world-class reception, and the American people will love you!"

"Great! Now let me get back to bed. We have plenty of time to implement our plan."

"Of course, I have one more thing I need to discuss, though."

"What is that?"

"Well, we have just received some intelligence reports that some domestic terrorist groups are working in the country against me. They do not want to see me retain power and are coordinating a possible attack once I retain the presidency.

"We can easily squash the rioters and protestors, but I do not want to have a well-coordinated response against me. It will show me as a weak and unprepared leader."

"Yes, that is troubling. I will send you some of my best intelligence agents to assist you in finding these groups. We have some capabilities that you do not have. They will easily find these groups and take them out before they become a threat to us."

"That would be great! I will give them clearance so they can get into the country. We can set them up here in the White House so I can have direct access to them."

"No, that would draw too much attention. I will have one of my agents already on the inside to be a liaison between you and them. For now, I want the agents to work from the outside; perhaps they can have access to your National Security Agency?"

"Yes, we can make that happen."

"Great, Dominik! I will send them in a few days."

"Perfect! Goodnight Vladimir. As always, you come through!"

President Vil hung up the phone, standing to look out the windows of the Oval Office. Staring at the Washington Monument in the distance, Vil felt he would soon stake his claim as the greatest president in history!

CHAPTER 9

STATE OF EMERGENCY

"HISTORY, IN GENERAL, ONLY INFORMS US WHAT BAD GOVERNMENT IS."

— THOMAS JEFFERSON

Tuesday, December 15th, 2020

"This morning, we bring you our ongoing coverage of the election fallout. Later in the hour, we will bring you an exclusive interview with a leader who claims he is part of a resistance movement to remove President Vil and restore democracy. We are also covering the latest numbers on the second wave of the 'Social Distance Pandemic' that took the world by storm last spring and is now posing a serious problem once again as a major health and economic crisis. Speaking of an economic crisis, the president tweeted this morning that he will address the nation tonight regarding actions the federal government will be taking against China for meddling in our election."

DE FACTO STATE OF WAR

December 15th, 2020

Conrad had finally made it home after what he considered one of his most difficult days since becoming a teacher. Last night his students heard through news outlets and social media that President Vil had officially been re-elected as president. Throughout the day, many students asked him questions about the constitutionality of this vote, the consequences, and about the still-pending Supreme Court decision regarding the outcome of the election.

Unfortunately, he did not have comforting news to tell them. It broke his heart to tell them that against all the odds, enough electors changed their votes to instill the presidency back to President Vil. He knew they had been swayed by all the confusion and chaos going on at the moment, but to defy not only the popular vote but for several of them to defy their state's popular vote, left him questioning the future of the nation.

He felt worried for his students, many of which were fearful of a more emboldened President Vil becoming even more tyrannical now than he had his presidency, and full constitutional powers reestablished. Many of his students either came from countries with authoritarian regimes, or their parents did. All he could do throughout the day was comfort them and instruct them about the courageous actions of leaders throughout the nation's history that stood up against the 'status quo' to act and make a change.

Conrad changed out of his typical work attire and put on his gym clothes and running shoes. Conrad thinks his best when out on the run, and went to get fresh air and clear his mind. Halfway through his run, it began to rain; he found shelter under a picnic cabana at a nearby park. He waited out the storm sitting at the picnic table and listening to the rain. It reminded him of a moment during a deployment to Afghanistan twelve years ago.

A FLASHBACK

He had been deployed as part of a cryptologic support unit for a Navy SEAL team. They were there as a new unit to provide tactical level critical communications intelligence to the SEAL team they had been assigned to. The unit was established to ensure that each SEAL team was provided the best on-the-ground tactical support from cryptologic assets.

The night that Conrad remembered was when they had been sent on a mission to take out an opium drug lord. It started to rain heavily while they were en-route to the suspected site of the drug lord, but they were directed to continue their mission. Conrad was in an MRAP (Mine-Resistant Ambush Protected) vehicle that protected against IED's (improvised explosive devices) and mines.

He and his crew were in the back portion of the MRAP that had been satellite converted to support their cryptologic systems. A loud explosion came from what sounded like the front of their convoy.

Conrad could not see the explosion because he was in the back of the MRAP. Their driver told them that an IED had taken out the up-armored vehicle at the front of the convoy. Just then, gunfire seemed to come from every direction, it was an ambush. There were six soldiers in their MRAP, the driver, navigator, Conrad, two other cryptologists, and their interpreter, Mustafa Wali. They had trained for ambushes several times but had never experienced one for real. Their hearts were racing.

BACK TO REALITY

The rain finally stopped, the clouds lifted, and Conrad's memory of the past began to fade. His heart was racing, and feeling an oncoming migraine, he decided to dart for his house so he could take his medication and then prepare dinner. When he arrived back at the house and opened the front door, he was surprised to find his brother Atticus at home. It had been over a month since he had last seen his younger brother.

"We'll look whose back. How's my little bro?"

"It looks like someone was out running in the rain."

"It came out of nowhere. They weren't predicting any rain today."

"They also weren't predicting all this turmoil we are going through either," Atticus replied.

"Don't even get me started. I had to tell my students today that Vil is going to remain president."

"What about the Supreme Court decision, though?"

"I can't imagine that they have much power to overturn the election now. The electors have already voted, so if they invalidate that vote, then we will be in even more uncharted waters."

"Speaking of waters…I am only going to be home for a few days. We go back out to sea on Friday."

"Well, let's make the best of it then. Want me to order a pizza for dinner?"

"That sounds great, actually! I'm sick of all the rice and potatoes they serve when we are out to sea. I haven't had pizza in a long time."

"I will call it in."

"Ok, I'll just be here in the living room watching some television."

Conrad was happy to have his brother back in town, even if it was only going to be for a few days. After he placed the pizza order online, he took his migraine medication, showered, and changed into some comfortable clothing. Walking back out into the living room, he recognized the voice emanating from the television.

"Can you turn that off or at least mute it. I'm sick of listening to Vil."

"Yeah…sorry, I was just listening to Vil's latest announcement."

"What is he saying now?"

"He is placing more sanctions on China for their supposed 'election meddling' that we both know isn't true. He said that all trade will cease between our countries at the end of the year, and to some degree, improve our trade relations with Russia."

"He's really trying to sell this China narrative, isn't he?"

"I'm sure that he is really doing this for more political reasons. If he can convince companies to open up shop and create jobs back here, then it will help him gain even more popularity."

"You're probably right. But the last thing this country needs is more low-wage earner jobs. Not only that, but Americans also aren't going to buy a product for $10 that is made here in the states when they are accustomed to paying $2.99 for that same product."

"You're right as always big bro. Hey, on my drive home from the base; I saw a lot of security guards in parking lots. What's up with that?"

"Oh, there are a lot of businesses that have gone as far as hiring security guards to protect them from being looted. Our school district actually modified our winter break to start early… one whole day! So, I only have one school day left until our break. My principal thinks things will settle down during the break, but I'm not as hopeful."

"Well, starting your winter break is good for both of us now that I'm back. Maybe we can go snowboarding up at Big Bear on Thursday and get away from all of this for a day."

"That would be great actually, as long as we are back before the nightly curfew."

The two brothers spent the rest of the night discussing Atticus's interaction with his commanding officer, who had become increasingly more erratic. Atticus told his brother of instances where several officers were scolded in front of other members of the crew.

THE VERDICT IS IN

December 16th, 2020

Conrad arrived early to school for his last day of the semester. He anticipated the long break now more than ever. He was also happy to have his brother home, even if it was only for a few days. He unlocked his classroom and went right to his desk to start up his computer and then walked over to turn on the projector.

He wanted to verify that everything was working properly so that he could project a video onto the screen in the front of the class directly from YouTube. Today he was going to show his students Martin Luther King Jr's "I Have a Dream" speech. He wanted to leave his students going into the winter break with a sense of hope for the future before them.

"Umm, excuse me, Mr. Aug, do you have a second?" asked Miguel.

"Yes, please, come on in Miguel," replied Conrad, pointing toward a desk encouraging him to sit down.

"This is just going to take a second, actually."

"What is it, Miguel?"

"Did you hear that the Supreme Court has made a decision regarding the president?"

"No, I haven't heard that. When did that happen?"

"While I was walking to school, my mother called to tell me that she saw it on the news. Mr. Aug, they have accepted what the president has been saying about the whole Chinese election meddling. They also said that because the electors voted in his favor, they cannot invalidate that decision.

"So he is going to be our president for another four years. Can you believe that? He actually succeeded in finding a way to work around our democracy to suit his need for power. My mother was right."

"I'm sorry to hear that the court chose not to uphold the Constitution. It seems that they waited to make a ruling to allow the electors to make the decision for them. Maybe this way, they could avoid being at fault for any fallout."

"This isn't the way our democracy is meant to work. I thought this country was a representative democracy. How is this representation of our nation?" Miguel replied.

"Well, it's actually...," Conrad paused.

He remembered back to his childhood when his father had countless conversations with him about the government. This conversation with Miguel made him recall one lesson very vividly. His father enjoyed reading and talking about the writings and speeches by several of the founding fathers, Alexander Hamilton, Thomas Jefferson, and George Washington, to name a few.

But one that his father always wanted to leave as a lasting impression on him as he grew from a child into adulthood was the one that resonated at the moment. It was the often-told story of Benjamin Franklin leaving the Constitutional Convention where he was approached by a woman who asked him what sort of government the delegates had created.

His response, although short, was significant. He told the group, "A republic if you can keep it."

Miguel, noticing that his teacher appeared to have drifted into thought, interrupted him.

"It's actually a what, Mr. Aug?"

"It's a republic…if we can keep it."

"I hope we can keep it. My uncle just told my mom last night that he was leaving for Idaho to join some resistance movement. He left this morning, and my mom thinks he won't be back."

"What resistance movement?"

"It's all over social media, Mr. Aug. Some groups are coordinating together to fight to keep President Vil from a second term. My mom believes they will all be slaughtered because they are going up against the government."

Before either of the two could say any more, the bell rang, signifying that the first period would begin in a few minutes.

"Ok, Mr. Aug, I'll see you in the seventh period," Miguel said as he left the class, fighting the incoming swarm of students.

As the day wore on, that childhood memory of his father telling him what Benjamin Franklin said played over and over in Conrad's head. Thankfully for him, his students were all engrossed in the speech by Martin Luther King Jr., so he was able to sit at his desk and think.

"Why did that particular moment in time become so important to me today?" he thought.

The country is falling into disarray. There is rioting daily. Multiple groups have vowed to fight Vil being sworn in for a second term.

There are numerous governors, senators, representatives, and state officials that are calling Vil's reelection unconstitutional and promising repercussions. Even some business leaders have now called out the president for acting outside the realm of the Constitution. But none of these people were doing anything with any unity. They were all just voices online and in the media.

That's when it dawned on him; he knew what he needed to do. There was no guarantee that his idea would work. But then again, he has made numerous decisions in his life that had no guaranteed outcome. He decided he had to act before it was too late. He crafted up his letter during his last class of the day. When the bell rang to let the students out for the winter break, Mr. Augustus signaled to Miguel Ruiz to stay behind and told everyone to stay safe and do their best to enjoy the holidays.

"Yes, Mr. Aug."

"Miguel, I'd like to thank you for becoming such an active learner in class. You are becoming a leader for your fellow classmates, and they look up to you. Take that with you wherever you go and wherever you end up in life."

"Ummm...well, thanks...Is everything alright?"

"I want you to be assured that people of good character will stand up to ensure our republic remains intact. I know you have your doubts, as does half this nation right now, as we find ourselves living in very troubling times. However, I think we look at this as an opportunity to recognize where we have faltered from our path and be able to find our way forward."

"I don't think I follow."

"Its okay, Miguel, you will, in time. Take care of yourself and your mother during the break."

A MOMENTOUS DECISION

Conrad got into his car, and before he turned the key to start the ignition, he texted his brother, ***Hey little bro, when I get home, we need to talk.*** He headed directly home, confident he had just made the right decision. When he got home, he found his brother doing laundry in preparation for his next at-sea deployment.

"Hey, what was that text all about?" Atticus asked.

"I don't think I'm going to be able to go snowboarding with you at Big Bear tomorrow."

"Oh, why not?"

"Well, I've realized that we are headed for some sort of major conflict, which might even lead to a civil war of sorts. Our nation is very quickly falling apart. We've got politicians openly talking about the possibility of a civil war, and that makes so many people very anxious about what is happening right now. I'm afraid without some sort of coordinated leadership, these groups that are recruiting people will end up just creating a big mess that will leave the vast majority of them either charged with treason or slaughtered."

"So, what is it that you are going to do? You're a history teacher."

"Not anymore."

"What do you mean?"

"I tendered my resignation to my principal today…effective immediately."

"What? Can you even do that? Why would you do that? What is it that you are you going to do now?" A concerned Atticus asked.

"I just feel that I need to get involved, and I explained my reasoning to my principal. He was very upset, but he understood what I have to do. Look, I realized, thanks to one of my students, that we can't stand on the sidelines when our nation is falling apart. We are on the brink of the end of our way of life, and if we do nothing, it will be lost forever.

"So, I am leaving for Sacramento tomorrow. Hopefully, I can talk to the one person that might be able to coordinate a response among patriotic Americans so that there is some organization to what we are on the verge of witnessing."

"And who exactly would that be?"

"Governor Perez. She has been a staunch critic of the president, and she is a very well-regarded leader."

Atticus replied with a snarky tone, "So she is just going to walk away from her position as governor and become some sort of leader in a resistance movement? Do you really think she's willing to risk committing treason against the nation?"

"She won't be committing treason. If she can compel enough people to stand up for the nation, then she could emerge as a leader of the resistance movement. The movement stands no chance without someone like her as their leader."

"Okay, you think that the governor of California is going to make time to talk with you? You are just going to drive up there and what...walk up to her secretary and ask for a meeting?" asked Atticus with a tone of sarcasm and disbelief.

"Well sort of, I actually know someone on her staff that owes me a favor."

"Who do know that works for the governor?"

"Mustafa Wali."

"Whoa!" replied a surprised Atticus. "Yes…I guess you could say he owes you a favor…or ten. What does he do for the governor?"

"He is her press secretary now. When she was an immigration lawyer, she helped him obtain his citizenship. It was the least our government could do after he spent several tours in Afghanistan as a translator for Special Forces teams. And they built a strong working relationship. She brought him on to her team when she became governor."

"And after you saved his life?"

"Yeah…I guess you could say that. But let's not go there; I get some really bad migraines every time I think about that."

"Fair enough, but I still think you should be talking to a professional about that Afghanistan experience."

"One day, I'm sure I will, but for now, I have a call to make and packing to do."

"Look, bro, I don't know what is going to happen in these coming weeks and months, …but you know I'm all in. I will provide any support that I can. If you need me to join you, I'll be right there by your side."

"Thanks, Atticus, but if anything, I need you on that ship."

"I'll have my satellite phone with me while we are at sea."

"Good. Okay, I've got to go make a call to Mustafa."

Conrad went to his room and grabbed one of his bags while he placed a call to his friend Mustafa. While he waited for his friend to answer, he realized he might need to grab a larger bag, but instead, he grabbed a few small bags and started packing some clothes.

"Hello, my friend. It has been too long. How are you doing?" asked Mustafa.

"I have been better, actually. What about yourself?"

"I'm sorry to hear that. Things are hectic up here. We have been extremely busy with this pandemic, not to mention the presidential election."

"Why would you be concerned about the presidential election?"

"Well, we are working with several cities to control the spread of violence. But it is really hard when we also have to deal with a health crisis that requires authorities to keep a distance from the protestors and rioters."

"That has got to be hard to manage."

"You have no idea, brother. So, to what do I owe the pleasure of your call?"

"I have a major favor to ask of you. I need you to put me on the governor's schedule for tomorrow or the day after."

"You think I can just snap my fingers and get you an appointment with the governor? It doesn't work like that. I don't even know why you want to see her."

"This is actually about the election. Look, I can't talk about this over the phone. I need you to trust me. You know I would never call in a favor if I didn't have good cause."

"Conrad, we have known each other for many years. I know you are a good man...in fact, I owe you my life. But you are asking me to schedule you to meet with Governor Perez tomorrow without telling me what this is all about."

"Yes! I can explain everything once I am there. I need you to trust me on this."

"Okay, here's what I can do. The governor is a busy woman, but she always makes time during lunch to respond to emails and letters from her constituents. I can tell her that you are a close friend and that as a favor to you, I would like for her to take a meeting with you during that allotted time."

"I just need thirty minutes."

"I definitely can't guarantee that much time, but I will do my best to get you a meeting with her. She owes me a favor anyway. Can you be here by noon tomorrow?"

"I can leave here early in the morning to avoid the Los Angeles rush hour."

"Good. Call me when you get here so I can bring you to the capitol. Don't be late. I'll see you tomorrow."

Conrad hung up the phone and finished packing his bags. He wanted to get to bed early to get a good night's rest so he could be up by 3 a.m. to get on the freeway for Sacramento, which is about an 8-hour drive.

CHAPTER 10

THE MEETING

"A REPUBLIC IF YOU CAN KEEP IT."

— BENJAMIN FRANKLIN

Thursday, December 17th, 2020. 12:02 AM

"This is your midnight news coverage, for all you insomniacs out there. Late in the evening, California, along with 17 other states, filed an emergency hearing with the Supreme Court to challenge the results of the Electoral College vote. Part of their claim is that the electors were swayed by yet-to-be proven allegations of Chinese election meddling, and that should not invalidate the votes of their citizens. Due to the extreme urgency of the case, we expect to hear later today whether the Supreme Court will take up the case."

OLD FRIENDS REUNITE

December 17th, 2020

Conrad woke up at the first sound of his phone's alarm. It was 2:45 a.m., and he needed to be on the road in fifteen minutes. He did not look forward to the drive ahead of him. He was thankful that he would have eight hours to craft a speech to the governor and go over it several times.

He put on his clothes, threw his bags in the backseat of his car, and backed out of the driveway. As he drove through his neighborhood, a feeling of acceptance came over him that he may never return to this place, he had come to call home. He quickly eliminated the thought from his mind to focus on preparing for his meeting with the governor.

He got a great head start to avoid the traffic in Los Angeles by leaving early. An hour north of the city, he stopped to fill up his gas tank and grab something to eat so he could have the energy to fuel him for the rest of the drive. The light from the sun began to peek over the mountains far off in the east as he got back on the freeway.

ANOTHER FLASHBACK

The mountains in the distance reminded him once again of the ambush in Afghanistan. The convoy had come under heavy fire from the mountainside surrounding them. Their driver and navigator both departed their MRAP to return fire. Conrad heard the heavy return fire and prepared the rest of his team to be ready to engage if they needed to get involved. Cryptologists are not normally engaged in combat by trade, but their work with Special Forces teams placed them in a nontraditional role.

All they could hear on their radios were directions between their unit that were being drowned out by heavy gunfire. Conrad heard a knock from the back of the MRAP. He knew it was someone on their team, but unsure if it was for additional support or to take in a wounded soldier.

BACK TO CONSCIOUSNESS

Conrad felt the tug of his steering wheel as he brought himself back to the present. His car had veered off to the side of the freeway and was rolling over the shoulder rumble strips. "I must have dozed off," he thought. He reached for the water bottle next to him and took a gulp. He became hyper-vigilant the rest of the drive to Sacramento. When he finally arrived at the capitol building, he felt prepared for his meeting with the governor. He reached for his phone to call Mustafa.

"Hey brother, are you here?" Mustafa asked.

"Yes, I just got here. I'm starving; let's get a bite to eat if there is time," Conrad replied.

"The governor is in a meeting at the moment, and I'm sure she will take a midday break for lunch after that. I know a place across the street where we can grab a bite before I take you to meet with her."

"Sounds great, I'll meet you outside."

Mustafa went promptly outside to meet his old friend Conrad. They both felt the urge to embrace each other since it had been so long, but they couldn't. The reemergence of the novel virus required everyone to keep a social distance of a few feet from one another. They proceeded to the bakery across from the capitol, and each ordered a croissant sandwich.

"How long has it been?" asked Conrad.

"Well, I think we last saw each other back at your retirement ceremony. No…wait…the last time was actually at my wedding."

"Has it been that long? That was five years ago, right?"

"Yes, next spring will be five years. We have two little ones running around the house now; a boy and a girl."

"Can I see their pictures?"

"Of course," replied Mustafa, reaching for his phone.

"Oh, look at them. They both have your eyes and your smile. What are their names and how old are they?"

"Alia, our girl, she is three. Conrad…our boy is thirteen months. We chose to name him after you."

Conrad looked up at Mustafa. He wondered how he had become so distant from his friend as to not know already. His military years seemed so distant to him at this point.

"I don't remember you telling me that."

"I know, I'm so sorry about that. My wife asked me several times to call you and let you know. I guess with this job…well, I've fallen into the American lifestyle of working endlessly. I didn't make time to call and let you know. I'm sorry."

"It's okay. We are here now, and that's what matters."

Mustafa, deciding to change the subject to avoid becoming overly emotional, and asked, "So, what is it that you want to talk to the governor about?"

"Let's talk about that inside."

When they got to Mustafa's office, Conrad asked, "Do you have a place where we can ditch our phones for the time being?"

"Yes, there are secure lockers in the governor's lobby."

"Perfect, let's get rid of these things, and then we can talk."

They placed their phones in a secure locker and then proceeded into Mustafa's office. Conrad closed the door behind him and searched the room to ensure there were no other electronic devices.

"Okay, this has got to be something serious," Mustafa said.

Conrad proceeded to tell his friend his fears about the probable fate of the nation and his belief that Governor Perez was one, if not the only, leader that could assemble and coordinate the resistance movement that had a chance to save the nation. Mustafa, feeling compelled to tell his friend everything that he knew about the governor's actions and the multiple resistance groups.

"Look, I'm probably not supposed to be telling you this, but over the last few weeks, the governor has been holding several meetings that have not been on her calendar, and I have not been privy to. I may not know exactly what those meetings are all about, but I do have a way of getting information.

"I don't have a full understanding of what is going on, but I have heard talk of cessation and also civil war coming out of these meetings. You might have shown up at the right time because I think the governor needs someone with a background in communications intelligence to help her, and whoever she is talking to, needs to be safeguarded better from monitoring by the Feds and the Russians."

Mustafa paused after hearing noises coming from the governor's lobby outside her office. He walked over to the door and peeked outside, noticing a few people that he did not recognize, and one person that he did, file out of her office. He closed the door, turning back to Conrad.

"It looks like the governor is done with her meeting. I saw former Secretary of State Johnson leaving her office. I wonder why he was in that meeting. Anyway, let me go check and see if she is ready to meet with you."

"Ok, let me spruce up really quick."

Mustafa headed for the governor's office. Conrad went over to a small mirror that hung on the wall and readjusted and tightened his tie so he could look professional. After he made sure he was presentable to the governor, he stared out the window, noticing the dark clouds roll in over the city. Mustafa returned after several minutes.

"Okay, she will meet with you, but she is only giving you fifteen minutes of her time."

"I guess I will need to prioritize my talking points."

The two friends proceeded into the lobby. Mustafa turned the knob to open the door to the governor's office, looking back at Conrad, who now looked quite pale. Conrad suddenly had a feeling of anxiety come over him as he followed behind Mustafa into the governor's office.

MEETING WITH THE GOVERNOR

"Governor Perez, I'd like to introduce you to my friend Mr. Conrad Augustus."

"It is a pleasure to meet you, Mr. Augustus," responded Governor Perez.

"Madam Governor, the pleasure is all mine," replied Conrad.

"I have heard great things about you. You are a former cryptologic technician, you worked with Special Forces, and now you are a high school history teacher. That's an impressive résumé and a noble career change."

"Thank you. It was a pleasure to serve my country. After settling in California, I felt that I could continue serving by working in my local community. Teaching high school kids has been an absolute joy, but sometimes it can be even more challenging than my work in the Navy, yet extremely rewarding."

"I can imagine. I would love to take some time to talk with you about your experiences in education at a future meeting. But, I've been told you have something more pressing to discuss with me today."

Conrad looked over at his friend Mustafa, hoping that he would start the conversation with the governor about his reasons for being there. Noticing the hesitation in Conrad, the governor motioned for Mustafa to leave the two so they could proceed.

"Thank you, Mustafa, for bringing your friend. Can you please call my husband and let him know that I will call him after I finish meeting with your friend?"

"Yes, Governor Perez. Conrad, I'll be in my office when you and the governor are done," replied Mustafa as he departed the governor's office.

"Thanks," Conrad replied.

"Okay, Mr. Augustus, what is this urgent meeting all about?"

"Please, call me Conrad. Before I tell you what brings me here, do you have a cell phone or any other electronic device with monitoring capability here in your office?"

"No. I actually leave my cell phone in my secure locker outside in the lobby during the day while I work. It helps me avoid distractions. "The only electronic device in here is that old fashioned clock sitting on my desk."

"Ok, good…so here's the thing…we've all seen the horrendous situation the president has put the nation in. This is well beyond the chaos that he has put everyone through since he was elected."

"You're right. In fact, it's completely unconstitutional."

"Exactly, we have seen the entire Republican side of the House and Senate move in lockstep with this president. They refuse to stand up to him, and that is how we have made it to this point.

"He used his 'fake news' propaganda to put the outcome of the election in dispute, which led several electors to defy their state's populace and vote for him. And now, the Supreme Court, after abdicating their responsibility to be that final check on our democracy until after the electors voted, rubber-stamped his second term."

"Well, we have actually challenged the results of the Electoral College and believe we have a strong case. So, what is it that brings you here to my office?"

"Ma'am, you may not want to hear this because it is something that I never envisioned would occur in our lifetime. Governor…we are in a de facto state of civil war."

"Civil war…how so?"

"These groups that have sprouted up all over the nation have vowed to not let the president retain control of the government and our democracy. The groups are growing in size every single day, and soon they will go beyond riots and eventually do something extreme. That will cause this president to use our armed forces on American soil against these groups, which will lead to millions of Americans being slaughtered."

"You give a very startling image of our future."

"That's why the nation needs you."

"Me? What can I do?"

"This nation needs a leader right now. She is screaming from the mountaintops for someone to stand up for those principles and beliefs that built this nation.

"She is telling us that our democratic way of life is on the verge of collapse, and if we don't act, then the nation…the democracy…our society…the government of the people, by the people, and for the people, SHALL perish from the earth."

"Well, I can see that the history teacher's blood runs deep in your veins."

"It is hard to be so deeply committed to this nation and not be willing to do something to save it. The nation needs you right now. You are the only voice of reason that has the ability to bring all of the resistance movements together. You can ensure the survival of our nation and help us remove this tyrant!"

Governor Perez spun her chair so that she could look out the large window behind her desk onto the grounds below. She needed to think about the unfolding events. As she stared out the window, she thought, "Can I trust this man? Who is he and why is he here at this very moment in time? What does he want out of this? Does he already know about some of the coordinated efforts being taken already? Did someone send him here to find out what I am involved with?"

"Conrad, I think you are right to be concerned. We definitely live in troubling times, and I appreciate your passion. But, I want to assure you that the safeguards of democracy will prevail. The Supreme Court will not defy the people because they know they have to substantiate our democratic principles, or else there is no democracy.

"The voice of the people will be heard, and our leaders will soon see the demands of the people, and they will do the right thing…if for no other reason than to ensure the sustainability of our democratic society that you are very passionate about."

"I don't think you…"

"You will have to excuse me, but I need to make a call to my husband, and I have several meetings that I need to prepare for. I do appreciate your passion. Your students are very lucky to have you as their teacher. It was a pleasure to meet you. Hopefully, one day after all the dust settles, we can talk about our education system and your experiences."

A now disheartened Conrad said, "Thank you, governor. It was a pleasure to meet you. Thank you for giving me some of your time. If I may leave you with one final thought that I tell my students at the end of each school year?"

"Of course, Conrad."

"When democracy dies in America, democracy dies everywhere."

Conrad departed the governor's office, and he found his friend Mustafa talking with a colleague in the lobby. He brought him up to speed on his conversation with the governor. Mustafa gave his condolences for things not working out. He walked him over to retrieve his phone. The two walked down the hall to the capitol entrance, where they departed, promising not to go as long between seeing each other again.

Conrad was exhausted from the early morning drive and decided to find a nearby hotel to check-in for the night. Even though it was only 1 p.m., he wanted to get a long rest before heading back home tomorrow.

Mustafa proceeded to his desk to finish a press release he had been working on with a deadline for later that afternoon. He typed up the final paragraphs of the release. While he proofread the entire document, he heard the sounds of footsteps approaching. He looked up to see who was approaching; to his surprise, it was the governor.

"Good afternoon, governor. I'm sorry if my friend got out of line or if what he felt to be appropriate for your level of attention should have been handled at a lower level."

"That's actually why I came to talk to you. Do you have a moment?"

"Of course, governor, let me just hit send on this press release. Okay, now I'm all yours."

"Come with me to my office. I need you to meet some people."

CHAPTER 11

IMMINENT CRISIS

"GOVERNMENT IS INSTITUTED FOR THE COMMON GOOD, FOR THE PROTECTION, SAFETY, PROSPERITY, AND HAPPINESS OF THE PEOPLE, AND NOT FOR THE PROFIT, HONOR, OR PRIVATE INTEREST OF ANY ONE MAN, FAMILY, OR CLASS OF MEN; THEREFORE THE PEOPLE ALONE HAVE AN INCONTESTABLE, UNALIENABLE, AND INDEFEASIBLE RIGHT TO INSTITUTE GOVERNMENT, AND TO REFORM, ALTER, OR TOTALLY CHANGE THE SAME WHEN THEIR PROTECTION, SAFETY, PROSPERITY, AND HAPPINESS REQUIRE IT."

— JOHN ADAMS

Thursday, December 17th, 2020

"Moments ago, President Vil tweeted out that he has accepted the resignation of the vice president today. This move was not expected and has caught us in the media, and I'm sure you at home, by surprise. Adding to that revelation, he has also now nominated his daughter to fill the role of vice president. Here are the tweets he issued to inform the nation:

@realDonaldEVil -- It is with great reluctance that I tell you that our vice president is stepping down immediately after serving, with high distinction, during my first term. He will return to private life, and the nation owes him a great deal of gratitude for his service. We will all miss him and everything he has done for the country over the last four years.

@realDonaldEVil -- I have nominated my daughter Sophia Kaiser to become my vice president during my second term. She is an incredibly successful businesswoman and will make our nation even better with the experience she brings! She will be fabulous! In fact, one day, she will make a great president!

"We are sure everyone wants to know what prompted the vice president to resign, or if he was forced out. The nomination of Vil's own daughter as the future vice president will surely spark controversy. This is breaking news, and we will continue to bring you updates as they develop."

MISSION FAILURE

December 17th, 2020

After checking into his hotel room, Conrad took a long hot shower before settling into the queen-sized bed. He was ready to take a short nap before wandering out to grab some dinner. While he sat there, trying to fall asleep, he noticed a loud noise outside. He got up from the bed to peek out the hotel window and investigate the noise. He discovered a large contingent of soldiers in Humvees driving down the main street adjacent to the hotel.

"It looks like they have finally made their way to California to start enforcing this curfew," Conrad thought.

Walking back to the bed, he decided he should bring his brother up to speed on his meeting with the governor. Atticus would be heading out to sea tomorrow, and it might be the last time he could communicate with him for a while. He grabbed his phone from the nightstand where it had been charging and sent him a text.

Meeting with Gov P didn't work out well. It seems she still has faith in the system or afraid I might be a spy.

His brother replied, almost immediately. ***Sorry to hear that. What will you do now?***

I guess I will look into one of these groups. They will need someone with my type of background to have any chance of success to assure their secrecy with my cryptologic background.

You are really going to join one of these groups? You are risking jail or worse.

And if I do nothing, what then, this is bigger than me? The checks and balances our leaders always praise in the constitution didn't work. This is about the future of democracy, not just in our country but the entire world.

I understand. Let me know what I can do from the inside. I'm still with you on this. I believe you are on the right side of history, and I want to be part of it as well.

Thanks, bro. Stay safe while at sea, and hopefully, we will see each other soon.

Oh, did you hear that the VP resigned today, and Vil nominated his own daughter to replace him?

Kidding right?

Sadly I'm not. I wish I was!

I haven't been monitoring any news alerts all day. The nerve of this guy to turn this into his own family business, gonna take a nap, I will text later.

Conrad put his phone back on the nightstand and quickly dozed off. After two hours of much-needed rest, he was awakened by the sound of yelling voices coming from the next room. He couldn't make out what was being said, but he could tell the people in the other room were upset about something. Unable to get any more rest, he turned the television on to catch up on the latest news. That was when he realized what the people in the next room were probably yelling about.

He read the breaking news bulletin that scrolled across the bottom of the screen. **Supreme Court refuses to hear an election case brought by the states.**

Conrad was no longer shocked by the never-ending dreadful news, but he was still upset with the decision. He put on some clothes and headed out of the hotel to find a place that was open so he could get a meal to bring back to his room.

As he walked down the street, he passed by several restaurants that he assumed would normally be quite busy around this time, but instead was almost empty. He noticed a small taco shop at the corner, which made his stomach growl. He could definitely satisfy his hunger with some street tacos and carne asada fries. He walked inside, where he found only one worker, which turned out to be the shop's owner.

"Hello there. Do you have carne asada fries?" asked Conrad.

"Of course we do," replied the store owner.

"Can I get three tacos de adobada and order of the carne asada fries?"

"Coming right up," the man said as he walked over to the grill to prepare Conrad's order.

"How bad have the riots and curfew been for business?"

"Oh, it's absolutely killed the business. I had seven employees working for me; I had to lay them off. I barely get enough business to justify staying open anymore. If this lasts much longer, then I'll have to shut down for good."

"I'm sorry to hear that. I hope things settle down soon so the business can come back for you, and you can hire your employees back."

"That would be great, but with this president running the country, we will probably have this chaos last for several years," the man said as he finished preparing Conrad's order and handed it to him.

"How much do I owe?"

"That'll be $14.69."

Conrad reached into his wallet to grab his credit card. Before he pulled his card out, he remembered that he had two one hundred dollar bills in there. He pulled the two large bills out and handed them to the man.

"Your total was only $14.69," the man said, staring at the two large bills.

"Keep it. These are hard times, and I can afford to part with it."

"Thanks, man. Hey, want a margarita to take with you? I make them in house, and I can make a whole pitcher for you to take."

"Sure, with my day, a pitcher worth of margarita would definitely take the edge off."

"Coming right up."

The man went to the back of the kitchen and prepared a margarita in a large pitcher for Conrad. Conrad thanked the man and wished him well with his business, given the circumstances. Conrad returned to his room, downed the three tacos along with three glasses of margarita. He felt his phone vibrate and pulled it from his pocket to find a new text from his brother.

Turn on the news. This may be the straw that breaks the camel's back. There is definitely no turning back now.

Conrad wondered what the mysterious text was all about, but that mystery quickly faded away. The breaking news was on every channel. **Speaker of the House arrested on charges of treason!**

"I think it's time for another drink! How can anyone believe this crap? How are people so blind to this? Or maybe they have just become numb to all this craziness. This is just too unreal to really be happening in 2020!" he exclaimed out loud as he made fists with his hands and shook them over his head in anger.

He downed the rest of the margarita and passed out around 7 p.m.

A KNOCK AT THE DOOR

December 17th, 2020

Conrad's arm jerked suddenly, causing him to wake up from a deep sleep. Unaware of what caused his sudden return to consciousness, he looked around the hotel room. His body was covered in a cold sweat, body shaking, heart-pounding, and his left arm had gone numb. He must have had a nightmare that startled him awake, but he could not recall it. Then he heard the loud pounding coming from his hotel room door.

"Who could that be, and why are they pounding on the door like they are they the police?" he thought.

Conrad got up from the bed and cautiously walked to the door. Peering through the peephole, he saw several men in dark suits outside.

"Is this, what woke me up? How long have they been here? Who are they and what do they want?" he thought.

Conrad, stuttering, finally said, "Can…I…help you?"

One of the men replied, "Is this Mr. Conrad Augustus?"

"Yes. What is this about?"

"We were sent by Governor Perez. She would like to meet with you immediately."

"Were these men really sent by the governor? What if these men are Federal Agents and this is a rouse to get me to open up the door to detain me?" Conrad thought.

Realizing he had no way to escape, he slowly unlocked and opened the door, hoping that they were not Federal Agents. One of the men pushed through the door and held it open, while the four other men in suits pushed passed Conrad, storming the room.

"What is this all about?" asked Conrad.

The man at the door did not respond. He was scanning the room and waiting to get the 'all clear' signal from the other men. Conrad turned and saw the men combing over every part of the room.

"All clear," the man at the door said into a small lapel microphone attached to his suit after receiving the 'all clear' from the men in the room.

Conrad stepped back from the door, not knowing what to expect next, his heart racing. The men departed the room, and within a few seconds, he saw Governor Perez appear at the doorway.

"Governor…what, are you doing here?" asked Conrad.

"Hello, Mr. Augustus. When we spoke earlier today, I was skeptical of your motives. I knew very little about you and with everything going on at the moment, there is plenty of reason for me to be cautious. Imagine my shock when someone walks into my office, telling me that the nation is headed toward civil war, and they need me as their leader."

"Well, I don't trust a lot of politicians. I'm sure you know that most of them are crooked. But I did my research on you when you were running for governor. Your story is quite compelling, and you have been true to your word...someone this country needs right now."

"Look, we can't talk here, I'm fairly sure that I have been under surveillance for a while now. When you came into my office, I had to assume you were a spy. I have a lot to catch you up on, but we can't do that here. Grab your belongings, and let's head back to the capitol. We can talk on the ride back."

Conrad quickly threw his belongings into his bags and then headed outside with the governor, surrounded by her security detail.

"Well, this is quite the security detail. I didn't realize a governor would have as much security as the president," mocked Conrad, noticing the rest of her security detail and a six-vehicle convoy that accompanied the limousine.

Governor Perez laughed. "Yes, my security detail has been doubled since last week. We can talk inside the limo. The back portion was designed to be soundproof and impenetrable by radio waves.

"We can talk in there without the worry of being monitored. Just hand your electronic devices over to the head of my security detail and get in."

Conrad handed over his cell phone to the head of the security detail and then got into the limo. This was much different than any limo he had been in before, it felt much smaller. He assumed that was due to the armor and technology upgrades to make it meet their security needs. He then noticed his friend Mustafa sitting at the far end of the inside. They both gestured in acknowledgment of each other.

"Conrad, I'm going to get right to business. The Speaker of the House contacted me several weeks ago to inform me of intelligence reports she had received of the president working with the Russians for several years. She also informed me that the president has been orchestrating an attempt to take over the government entirely."

"You mean install himself as an authoritarian leader?"

"Basically, he has slowly been dismantling the government from within, under the guise of 'draining the swamp.' Now, he is planning to use all of these simultaneous crises to increase the powers of the executive office and render the other branches of government effectively useless. His own party refuses to stop him because they are just as power-hungry as he is. Although many of them do not agree with him, they are tied to him because they know they must stand by his side if they want to implement their own goals."

"So why are you telling me all of this now? Just a few hours ago you told me that 'the safeguards of democracy would prevail.'"

"Let me explain that. Several other governors, politicians, business leaders, and yes, even leaders of most of the resistance groups, have been coordinating under my leadership to devise a plan to take our country back. In fact, right before you came into my office, I was meeting with several of our key leaders. Over recent days we have concluded that the only way to remove this 'illegitimate occupant' of the White House from power is to declare war against him."

"You mean a civil war?"

"No, we are not declaring war against half the nation. Vil is the threat to our democracy, and therefore we will be declaring war against him and him alone."

"You do realize that he has the strength and power of the entire federal government at his fingertips? He can use that to crush any resistance movement against him. Plus, a majority of his faithful followers will certainly be willing to pick up arms to protect him and keep him in power. He has created a cult-like following, and when people join a cult, they lose their sense of reality and common sense."

"Yes, we do recognize that as a strong possibility. If people are willing to fight against their own democracy for an authoritarian leader, then we will have to fight them too. We also believe we can incentivize democracy-loving citizens to fight on our side as well. We are working to bring the necessary arms, ammunition, and technology to go up against whatever Vil throws at us."

"That is quite a daunting task. You are going to need the help of other countries to get all of the necessary arms and…never mind, I'm sure you already know that. But that still doesn't explain why I am here."

"You're right; it doesn't, and so let me explain. After you left my office, I spoke with former Secretary of State Johnson about our meeting. He has been coordinating things at the national level for us. He has effectively become number two in this endeavor to save the nation."

"Like your vice president?"

"No. We are not seceding from the Union; we are saving it. Since you are a history teacher, I'm sure you understand and appreciate the difference."

"Of course, so, I guess then that makes you the leader of the resistance, and he is the vice-leader."

"I'd like to think that this is the movement to restore democracy. I'm sure we will figure out a proper name to call what we are undertaking, but that's not incredibly important right now. Anyway, Secretary Johnson used his resources inside the Pentagon to do a background check on you.

"Surprisingly, it didn't take long. Secretary Johnson's contacts claim you are one of the best when it comes to information warfare and cryptology. He read over your file and was impressed. He urged me to bring you on board the...'resistance.' So, I pulled Mustafa into my office and brought him up to speed on what I have kept him in the dark about over these last several weeks."

"And, Governor, I appreciate your trust in me," Mustafa interrupted.

"I'm sorry for not bringing you into the fold earlier, but all of the leaders have agreed to keep this to a limited group for now," she replied.

"We are all on the same page and will have to be together on this from now on," Mustafa stated.

"Indeed, we do; and thank you for connecting your friend Conrad with me," she began. Looking back at Conrad, she continued, "Conrad, after I brought Mustafa up to speed, I told him that none of our plans have a chance of success without a successful information warfare mission so that we can conduct the psychological operations, cyber-warfare, military deception, electronic warfare, and operational security components during the initial phase and continuing phases of our operations. He was quick to speak up for your expertise. He told me that if we bring you onboard, we will have the best chance of fighting this war to save the nation and our democracy.

"In fact, he said you are the only person he trusts to be able to accomplish this piece of our mission. He also told me what you did for him in Afghanistan, and frankly, I now feel embarrassed that I did not trust you before."

Conrad interrupted, "I appreciate my friend for speaking so highly of me. I can assure you that he probably embellished things a bit."

Governor Perez replied, "I doubt that, Conrad. But I do appreciate your modesty. You have the experience and knowledge of the capabilities and limitations of what we are going up against. We need an expert in information warfare to develop a strategy for us to prepare our battle space for war.

"We have to get out ahead of things because we will be going up against the might of the entire federal government and its vast resources. If we develop a strong information warfare campaign at the beginning, then we stand a chance to take back our nation. If not…then I'm afraid we might just be a bunch of citizens running around with pitchforks against the strongest military in the world. Will you join our team?"

"Yes! You can count me in! We will win this fight because the American people are counting on us. The fate of democracy is counting on us. History is counting on us."

"That's great news! We are almost back to the Capitol building. I will inform each of our regional leaders that we now have someone to coordinate our information warfare campaign. I will set you up near the Capitol in a bunker room in an abandoned office building that I want you to turn into your classified workspace.

"I will send my commanding general over tomorrow to meet with you and bring you up to speed on our current operational plans. I will also lend you an aide that is fully up to speed so you can have someone to assist you in developing your plan and coordinating that with the general."

"That's great, but if I am going to plan something of this scope and magnitude, I am going to need my team to join me on this."

"Your team?" the governor asked.

"Yes. The team will consist of my closest colleagues from my Navy days and the best in the field. We are going to need them if we want to win this fight. I trust every one of them with my life, and I can assure you that they will be fully onboard. They have been just as ashamed of the changes Vil has made, and his authoritarian power grabs."

"Then I will take you at your word. How many of these colleagues are on your team?"

"There are seven of them."

"Okay, when we get done here, give their information to the head of my security detail, and I will have him send for them to be brought here."

"Sounds good governor, and they all live right here in California, so I would like them here by the weekend. I will let them know to expect visitors in suits to be knocking on their door, so they aren't caught off guard like I was."

"And how will you do that? We are all quite paranoid about our phones being monitored at this point. We only have a limited supply of encrypted satellite phones at the moment. We are working on getting some more, but that will be a while."

"Don't worry; we have a backchannel in case of emergency. The Feds won't be able to track our communications." Conrad replied.

A puzzled Governor Perez replied, "Okay, I will leave that to you."

Mustafa interrupted, "Governor, we are here. Conrad, whatever you need we will get for you, just let me know."

"Thank you, my friend. Once I see this office, I'm sure I will have a whole list of needs to ensure that we can't be monitored by the Feds or anyone else," stated Conrad.

"Oh, one last thing," said Governor Perez, "we will need a fully coordinated and developed plan by the end of the year. I will expect daily updates from either you or someone on your team."

"I guess I won't be sleeping much over the next two weeks then. You politicians love your meetings as much as the admirals and captains I use to work for loved them. Don't worry, we will make sure you are briefed daily and that we are aligned with the plan your general is developing."

The three parted ways. Governor Perez and her press secretary headed inside the capitol building. Conrad was escorted by a member of her security detail to his new basement office in an empty building, a few blocks away.

He put together a list of the requirements to convert the office into a SCIF (sensitive compartmented information facility) to prevent any potential monitoring from the Feds and the Russians. The office needed to be soundproof and impenetrable by radio waves so that he could not be monitored.

CONRAD SETS UP BASE OF OPERATIONS

December 19th, 2020

Conrad converted his office space in the basement of the large vacant office building a block away from the Capitol building, into what he now called his new headquarters, and quickly got to work. He had one of the governor's aides assigned as a permanent assistant to him, and he put the aide to work right away.

They converted the space with the help of the members of his newly created team as they arrived. Thanks to Mustafa's help in acquiring the tools and materials, they completed the project in less than two days. After the SCIF was set up, Conrad got to work crafting his first draft of the plan while waiting for the rest of his team, which would arrive shortly. He had promised the governor that he would have a plan completed by December 31st, which left him less than two weeks to complete. He brought each member of the team up to speed as they arrived. The task before them was extremely daunting, but he knew this particular group was up for the challenge.

CHAPTER 12

INFORMATION WARFARE

"THE PEOPLE CANNOT BE ALL, AND ALWAYS, WELL INFORMED. THE PART WHICH IS WRONG WILL BE DISCONTENTED IN PROPORTION TO THE IMPORTANCE OF THE FACTS THEY MISCONCEIVE. IF THEY REMAIN QUIET UNDER SUCH MISCONCEPTIONS, IT IS A LETHARGY, THE FORERUNNER OF DEATH TO THE PUBLIC LIBERTY. ... WHAT COUNTRY BEFORE EVER EXISTED A CENTURY AND A HALF WITHOUT A REBELLION? AND WHAT COUNTRY CAN PRESERVE ITS LIBERTIES IF THEIR RULERS ARE NOT WARNED FROM TIME TO TIME THAT THEIR PEOPLE PRESERVE THE SPIRIT OF RESISTANCE? LET THEM TAKE ARMS. THE REMEDY IS TO SET THEM RIGHT AS TO FACTS, PARDON, AND PACIFY THEM. WHAT SIGNIFY A FEW LIVES LOST IN A CENTURY OR TWO? THE TREE OF LIBERTY MUST BE REFRESHED FROM TIME TO TIME WITH THE BLOOD OF PATRIOTS AND TYRANTS."

— THOMAS JEFFERSON

Monday, December 21st, 2020

"We have just learned that the incoming Republican-controlled House of Representatives and Senate will vote on January 3rd to confirm President Vil's daughter Sophia as vice president. There was some confusion as to whether she was eligible to hold the office because her residence was also New York, the same as her father. The Constitution specifically states that the president and vice president shall not be inhabitants of the same state.

That was cleared up last night after we were informed by the White House that Sophia Kaiser had changed her residency to Washington D.C. when she and her husband moved there at the beginning of the president's first term when she became a senior advisor to the president. This will make her the first family member to become a vice president to a president in our history."

THE PLAN DEVELOPS

December 21st, 2020

Conrad and his team of seven friends and former cryptologists were hard at work, crafting an information warfare plan. His friends had arrived throughout the weekend, and he quickly put them to work. He assigned each of them to a specific mission area. They conducted numerous briefings each day to keep themselves on track and aligned with everyone else. They were on a deadline, and Conrad always met his deadlines.

At their final briefing for the day, Conrad told the group that the plan they were finally developing would require outside assistance. Their plan was very robust but would not be successfully executed without the assistance from businesses in the telecommunications, entertainment, media, and technology innovation sectors.

He was reluctant to bring in more help, especially from outside of his trusted circle, but he knew this mission required it. After the meeting, his most trusted colleague and friend, Jasmine Williams, pulled him aside to explain the scope of the assistance they needed. Jasmine was a former sailor that had worked for Conrad in their Navy days. She was the best cryptologist Conrad ever met during his career. The field was heavily dominated by men back when he served, and Jasmine was an African American woman in a 95% male-dominated field.

She never let her status as a woman hinder her success, and she never tolerated any negative energy. She simply did her job and did it well. Conrad was not happy to see her leave the Navy to pursue another path, but he knew she would be successful wherever she went. She did exactly that. After leaving the Navy, she became a successful entrepreneur, founding a cybersecurity firm.

"Conrad, if we are talking about being able to conduct a plan of this nature, then we will need outside help. There is just no way that we can conduct an operation of this size and scope without assistance from certain segments of the business community. We are talking about conducting psychological operations, cyber warfare, military deception, electronic warfare on a massive scale, the likes of which have never been done before.

"And we are doing all of this while also protecting a group of mostly untrained and uncoordinated civilians that have no understanding of operational security. We are going to have a lot of training to do," stated Jasmine.

"I know…you're right. That means that we will have to bring more people into the loop, and then I want to," replied Conrad.

"We aren't going to have a choice. We are talking about conducting operations that are outside the scope of our capabilities. They have the technology and personnel to conduct the things we are planning, especially when it comes to hacking telecommunications and power grids."

"Let me talk to the governor. I'll need not only her permission but probably her influence on this. We will have to convince several companies to aid this effort, and we don't even know their politics, not to mention the numbers of employees these companies have that we will have to bring into the loop. We'd have to ensure that they are all on board. Let me bring her up to speed."

A COORDINATED EFFORT

December 22nd, 2020

"Governor, thank you for coming over," Conrad said.

"We are all quite busy right now, but you said this was urgent. We've got several governors on board and willing to bring all of their resources to this. We've also been in talks with several of the resistance groups to bring them all into the fold under one coordinated leadership. Everything seems to be coming together quite nicely. So what is it that you need?"

"That's good news. We are working diligently here to complete the information warfare part of the plan. We have been coordinating with your commanding general, but we have come across a point where we need your position and influence if we are going to move forward."

"I'm listening." Governor Perez replied.

"We are going to need the assistance of these companies," Conrad said, pointing to the whiteboard in front of him, "If we are to implement our plan."

Conrad laid out the plan for the governor so she could understand the full scope of the coordination they would need. He explained to her his uncertainty with bringing these companies on board because of the risk of the information, making it outside their control and into the hands of the president. The governor, however, did not share the same skepticism. She informed him that she would send for the CEO's of these companies so they too could be brought into the loop.

"Conrad, don't worry about this list; I'll take care of getting the leaders of these companies here. Use your team to convert this entire building into a SCIF so we can have as much of the team working from here going forward. I'll have everyone on this list here by…noon tomorrow."

"That's pretty quick, but we will get it done. But how are you so sure that these CEO's are going to be willing to work with us?"

"You don't become the governor of a state with the 5th largest economy in the world without working with most of the businesses on your list. I know most of the leaders of these companies personally. It is safe to say that most of them have already been working with us in some capacity. Our goal is one and the same…save our democracy."

"If you are already working with many of them, then this might not be as hard as we envisioned."

"Don't be so optimistic just yet. I've been looking over your plans, and I can't say that everyone is going to be willing to increase their involvement in the scale you are requesting. So, have a good pitch ready to go tomorrow. None of these business leaders are going to be happy about being brought here on such short notice. It'll be incumbent upon both of us to sell this to them. They will need to understand how this affects the nation and why we can't do this without them."

THE PLAN IS COMPLETE

December 31st, 2020

Conrad emerged after almost two full weeks of being locked down in his bunker-like headquarters. He stepped outside the building, flanked on both sides by his closest friends and former colleagues. It was time for them to reveal the plan they had developed in close coordination with the governor's military chiefs and a vast network of business leaders. It was his first time seeing the brightness of the sun since his team had arrived.

He managed to convince the majority of the business leaders to join the effort. He was surprised at how easily the majority of them were willing to participate and bring their businesses and talent to this major endeavor. The few that were reluctant to get involved were swayed by the peer pressure they received from their business leader counterparts.

In total, over 300 people were brought in to ensure the plan was developed successfully. Everyone was required to hand over all of their electronic devices before they could join the team. They even had to sleep in the building, which they had converted an entire floor into a makeshift barracks to house everyone. The first night he saw CEOs sleeping in cots right next to their employees, he felt in his gut that the nation could possibly be saved.

Now it was time to take their plan to the governor. She had given them a deadline of the end of the year, and they had successfully met that deadline, barring any changes. His team headed for the Capitol building to present their plan. There was little time left before things begin to roll into action, and their piece of the plan would allow everything to proceed.

They arrived at the capitol just as several other leaders were arriving. Their presentation was scheduled to be the first briefing before the group. Conrad's biggest concern was electronic surveillance of the meeting, so they had ensured that every one of these leaders disposes of any electronic form of communication for the next several weeks.

This would present a possible problem with coordination. Still, it had to be done to prevent monitoring by the Feds and especially the Russians. They walked into the room, where several governors and the resistance leaders awaited to hear how they would proceed to take back the nation from the illegitimate President Vil.

THE INFORMATION WARFARE PLAN

The following plan has been redacted and to be read by Governor Perez's eyes only. No matter how secure our operation is, we still worry about leaks.

CHAPTER 13

UNRESTRAINED

"HOW STRANGELY WILL THE TOOLS OF A TYRANT PERVERT THE PLAIN MEANING OF WORDS?"

— SAMUEL ADAMS

Friday, January 1st, 2021

"We have some major breaking news to bring you this morning. We are tracking two developing stories related to the Supreme Court that are just devastating for the country right now. We have just learned that Justice Esther Goldberg has passed away in her home of apparent natural causes; she was 89 years old. She had a long legacy of fighting for civil rights, and she will be missed.

We have also just learned that Justice Andrew Stephenson has been diagnosed with the novel virus that has taken the lives of so many around the world. He has been taken to a local hospital in Washington, D.C., so he can get breathing assistance through the use of a ventilator. I will also receive around the clock monitoring; he is 83 years old.

Both Justice Goldberg and Stephenson are the most liberal-leaning justices on the court. With the passing of Justice Goldberg, that leaves a vacancy that will most undoubtedly be filled by President Vil with a conservative judge, making a 6-3 conservative Supreme Court.

In the unfortunate event of Justice Stephenson also passing, then we could very well end up with a conservative 7-2 Supreme Court. This might create a conservative court for an entire generation, which could lead to the overturning of major decisions that have advanced our civil rights on many issues. We will continue to bring you the latest news as these stories continue to develop."

DAUGHTER SOPHIA SWORN IN AS VICE PRESIDENT

January 3rd, 2021

President Vil sat at the resolute desk in the Oval Office, plotting his next moves. Two of the most liberal Supreme Court Justices passed away in the last 48 hours. Justice Goldberg died of natural causes in the early morning hours of the New Year, and Justice Stephenson died late last night of complications from the novel virus. His daughter Sophia will be confirmed by the new House of Representative and Senate later today and be sworn in as the new vice president. He felt that everything was coming together better than planned.

He could now ensure that everything would work to benefit him and his ally, Russian President Vladimir Porchensky. With a majority in both chambers of Congress, he would be able to push through an agenda that would give him more powers and eventually render the legislative branch powerless. Once he has his 7-2 conservative Supreme Court installed, then he will no longer have to worry about his agenda being slowed or even stopped by the court.

With the country in chaos, in only a few shorts weeks, he will be able to consolidate enormous powers in his hands. Then he will have the ability to use the military to crush the resistance groups and become a hero to his followers that he so desperately wants. He can then focus his attention back on the dismantling of the government from the inside. World leaders will finally view the U.S. as a crumbling nation whose best days are in the past. This will make way for Russia to emerge as the new leader in the world, and Vladimir Porchensky as that global leader to follow behind.

It has been a bumpy road to get to this point. He had to utilize a strategy never before conceived in human history. It was one that involved manipulation and trickery from within the government.

He reckoned his trickery to that of the Wizard of Oz; "pay no attention to the man behind the curtain." He had successfully divided a nation and led the public astray, as Satan did to Eve in the Garden of Eden. This is his country now!

"Good afternoon, father. How do I look?" said Sophia as she twirled around in the custom-made designer dress that she will wear for her swearing-in ceremony later in the day.

"You look stunning, as always! You are going to make a great president replacing me one day after I die."

"Father, don't say such things. Once your second term is over, I will replace you, but you are still young and healthy. You will make it through another full term as president."

"Of course, I will! And once we take out these resistance groups, my popularity will soar through the roof. We will use that popularity to change the Constitution to eliminate the two-term rule, and with my popularity high, I will remain in power forever. And we always have the Russians to help us if we are ever concerned that anything will go against us. After 20 or maybe even 30 years of my rule, you will take over. No one will even be able to remember a day when the Vil's didn't run this country."

"You are such a genius father, but what about the media? They hate you, and they have tried to do everything to stop you from accomplishing your plans. Don't you think they will step up their attacks, and bring to light what we are doing?"

"I'm not worried about them anymore. I've been able to destroy their credibility by calling them 'fake news' and 'enemy of the people.'

"In fact, I will have their broadcast licenses taken away. Well, only the ones that spew that fake news. They should be singing words of praise about me; instead, they pick apart my words and analyze my actions. I will keep the ones that say only good things about me; they are the real news."

"Oh, father, you are always ahead of the game and so much smarter than everyone."

"And look at me now; I'm the most powerful person in the world."

"Yes, you are!" exclaimed Sophia as she looked down at her ringing phone. "Yes…oh perfect…well, we don't want to wait any longer, so let's get this show on the road."

"Did they finally vote?" President Vil asked.

"Yes, both chambers voted to confirm me as vice president."

"Let's go swear you into your new position as the second most powerful person in the world."

"And I'll be the most powerful woman in the world!"

They proceeded into the East Room, where a large group had assembled to witness the swearing-in of the president's daughter and first woman vice president. As this momentous occasion occurred, the onlookers seemingly acknowledged the unspoken truth that the president was, in fact, turning the presidency into an authoritarian regime. No one spoke a word of this out loud, for if anyone even is perceived as betraying him, they would feel his wrath.

The newly installed vice president spent the day celebrating with her guests. Her father gave her a spectacular ballroom event, which was streamed live on television for everyone to see. Vil wanted to normalize their roles as the dynasty he always envisioned, by continuously promoting themselves in front of the American people daily from this point forward. However, the party came to a quick end when they were summoned to the Situation Room for an emergency intelligence briefing.

A TRAITOR EXPOSES THE RESISTANCE

President Donald Vil, Vice President Sophia Kaiser, and her husband made their way to the Situation Room in the basement of the White House, escorted by several secret service agents. Sophia was upset that her first big moment in the spotlight had been cut short, and she demanded an answer as to why.

"I would like to know what this is all about. This is supposed to be my day!" exclaimed angry Sophia Kaiser.

"My apologies Madam Vice President, but we have some urgent intelligence reports that we need to brief you and your fa-…umm, the president on," replied President Vil's national security advisor.

"Go ahead, what is this all about?" asked President Vil, still a little upset from being whisked away from the party he had thrown for his daughter.

"We have recently come into contact with an American citizen who informed us of a coordinated plot to overthrow you. After we interrogated this individual for several hours, we were able to extract enough Intel from him that we know some of the participants."

"Who is trying to attempt a coup on my father?"

"Well, apparently, he was not high enough in the chain to know everything that they are planning. What he was able to tell us is that several governors are in their leadership ranks. He was also able to inform us that former Secretary of State Johnson is part of this planned coup. We believe that they are coordinating with many of the rioters to mobilize an attack and overthrow you by the end of this month.

"In order to uncover more details about their plot and to determine which governors are involved, we started monitoring their phones. We wanted to gather locational data on the governors and who they have been communicating with. What we learned from this is that we could not obtain active signals from the cell phones of 17 governors; they are all Democratic governors.

"The last time we were able to obtain signals from any of their phones dated back to December 30th, and for several of them, it goes back even further. We believe these are the governors involved in the planned coup," explained the national security advisor.

"They are all Democrats. They want to stage a political coup on you, father! They continue to refuse to accept the legitimacy of your reelection, and now they are willing to attempt to take you out."

"Well, I guess we will have to go round them up and arrest them for treason."

"It's not that easy, Mr. President. We don't actually know where any of them are located, and if they are coordinating a coup, they are practicing great operational security measures. We have stretched every resource to the maximum to locate them.

"Plus, we didn't obtain legal warrants to monitor their phones, so we would be on shaky ground trying to explain that to the courts. And most of the rioters have gone silent over the last few days, which leads us to believe they are planning a first strike very soon."

"Then I will just go on television and call every single one of them traitors and bring the people over to my side. They can't successfully accomplish a coup without the support of the people." Vil stated!

"Wait, father, I have a better idea. If you go on television and call them all traitors, then we get nowhere. Your popularity has always remained the same when you attack the naysayers, it may backfire. Let's try a different approach."

"What would that be, Sophia?"

"Let's declare war on China for their election meddling. You've already declared an economic war on them, now let's turn up the heat and declare a military war on them. This way, we get the people to rally around their president. Whenever a president has declared war, the people always support their president. We can kill their attempted coup before they even get a chance to implement it. The people will not tolerate overthrowing a wartime president."

"I love that idea. But you really want me to take the country to war with China? They have over a billion people. That would be a bloodbath."

"No father, we don't have to actually go to war with them. We just get the American people on our side and the Chinese to be on guard. We turn up the heat on the Chinese a little bit with increased troop movement.

"That will bring them to the negotiating table because they do not want to ruin their economy by going to war with the United States. It would be an endless war. Then we find some sort of reconciliation with them; both leaders get tons of publicity in front of the cameras shaking hands with each other, and poof…you become the president that everyone wants to reelect again and again."

"That's brilliant! I will go down in the history books as the greatest president in history!"

"We can use a wartime authorization to guarantee your executive powers that will be so broad you will have the power to do almost anything you want."

"I taught you so well, Sophia. You will follow in my footsteps and make a great leader and a great first woman as president."

That night, they crafted up the plan to give the president near limitless, unchecked powers to conduct war abroad against any enemy and on American soil against any group deemed as traitors to the nation. They had control of both chambers of Congress and would have no problem getting it passed quickly.

THE EMBOLDENED TYRANT

January 4th, 2021

President Vil woke up energized to implement the plan that was crafted late at night. He had a very busy day ahead of him with several announcements. First, he will announce to the American people that the nation will go to war with China.

He felt confident that after his announcement, the citizens will rally around him. This move would undoubtedly suppress any attempt at a coup. He was also ready to name two new justices to the Supreme Court today. One was his former personal lawyer and political fixer and the other his younger sister, who is the Chief Judge for the Second Circuit Court of Appeals, located in New York. During any other time, these two controversial nominees would never get approved. But the president had the unwavering support of the Senate, and he knew anyone he nominated would easily make their way onto the court.

Finally, he will have dinner with Senator McDaniel where he will inform him that due to the war, he will need Congress to vote to approve an amendment to the Constitution that eliminates the statute of limitations on the presidency and gives the president the power to indefinitely postpone an upcoming election when the nation is at war.

Something he knows will be easy to get passed through Congress but will be an uphill battle to get the states to ratify, but a fight he was ready to take on. At precisely noon, President Vil sat at the resolute desk, adjusted his tie, and prepared for the light on the camera to turn on so he could give his prepared remarks to the American people.

"My fellow Americans, our nation has come under attack by the People's Republic of China. We came under a deliberate and vicious cyberwarfare attack from an enemy that infiltrated our technological capabilities to conduct psychological operations upon our society. They tried to guarantee the outcome of our presidential election through the use of social media to dupe the American people into voting for their preferred candidate, my opponent. This is an act of war.

"We uncovered their scheme and have ensured that the true outcome of the election prevailed instead. If gone unchecked, this form of warfare will continue. They are already conducting this same form of warfare in numerous other elections around the world. I am hereby informing Congress to declare war against the People's Republic of China and grant me the powers to properly execute this war. We will win this war!"

The light on the camera went dark, and President Vil took a deep breath. In all the commotion of the last few days, he had forgotten to update President Vladimir Porchensky. He was sure that he would be upset to find out their plans after they were already in motion.

"Tonight, I will have to call Vladimir and smooth things out; I'm sure he will be disappointed that I did not inform him of this first. I will need him to talk with the Chinese leader to give him the assurance that we will not enact a real war, but we will mutually benefit from our nations rallying around their leaders," Vil said to his daughter.

Vil prepared for his next major speech, which would happen at 3 p.m., where he would announce his nominations to the Supreme Court. He went back upstairs to the residence to monitor how the media was reacting to his announcement. To his surprise, the major media outlets were condemning his announcement and demanding he provides proof of his claims.

Vil was furious because only his favorite news station was covering him with their normal praise. He grabbed the phone and demanded to be connected immediately with the head of the FCC (Federal Communications Commission), which oversees the broadcast media.

"Yes, Mr. President," answered the whimpering voice of the nervous FCC chairperson.

"I'm done playing games with the media. Revoke their broadcast licenses. I want them off the air, except, of course, the one that covers me well. The rest of them are just fake news! They should praise their leader like the media does in many other countries!"

"It doesn't quite work that way, it's more complicated than that."

"Look, these stations are spewing 'fake news' by not praising my leadership. I want every station's license revoked if they continue this misconduct! We are at war, and the nation must unite around their leader! If you can't do, then I will find someone who will!"

"Yes, Mr. President, I will see what can be done."

"I want them off the air before the end of the week."

"It doesn't work that quick."

"Then I want you gone. I'm sending my vice president down there to take swift action."

President Vil hung up the phone and then called his daughter up to the residence to inform her of his request for only positive news coverage to remain on the air. He told her that he wanted them off the air by the end of the week. His new vice president, who also hated the constant negative coverage of her father, quickly dispatched to carry out her father's request.

That afternoon, he officially nominated his former personal lawyer as well as his sister to the Supreme Court. He stated to the crowd of onlookers that he expected a quick confirmation process for both of them. Now it was time for his meeting with Senator McDaniel. President Vil had a plan in place to get the senator to push the amendment quickly through Congress and out to the states for ratification.

"Mr. President, it was great to see you nominate such strong conservative members to the court today," beamed an overjoyed Senator McDaniel.

"I'm glad you are pleased with my choices. After they are confirmed, we will have a conservative court for at least another 30 years, and we can ensure our political agenda is enacted," replied Vil.

"That makes everyone in our party very happy. We can begin to move legislation through the states and federal government that reflects our ideals. When they are challenged and work their way to the Supreme Court, they will be upheld, and we will finally have the conservative nation our forefathers envisioned.

"Forget those old fools. If they really wanted a strong government, they would have given more powers to the president. I wouldn't have to deal with all of these ridiculous fights with politicians if they would have given more power to the presidency."

"Well that is all part of the system of checks and balances, I'm sure you understand that."

"What I understand is that we are going to war, and this war will wage on for a long time. We need a consistent strong leader at the top, so I need to be granted more powers."

"Of course we do. You have just been re-elected for another four years, so we will maintain that consistency for quite a while."

"No, that won't be enough. It's time that we eliminate that ridiculous rule that limits how long I can stay in power."

"Well, let's be careful here. If you are talking about the amendment that limits a president to two terms, then we are talking about making a change that would be highly unpopular by my colleagues. That amendment was made because the same Democratic president was elected four times. He had so much power and popularity that he got almost everything he wanted, and our party became weak for many decades. We don't want to risk that happening again."

"Mitch, Mitch, listen here. We won't see that happen because I will be the one re-elected every time. The country loves me, and they love the show I put on for them. You can see it in the ratings every time I am on television. They think this is a reality show, and I have used my brand to really elevate the power of the presidency.

"I've made the presidency popular again. They will keep reelecting me, and then one-day …perhaps…my daughter. Okay, yes, my daughter will end up as our next president. We will run this country for so many years that this nation will want the Vil's as their leaders for generations to come. Look, if we work together, we can even eliminate the Democratic party."

"Even if I can get this passed through the Congress, it still has to be ratified by three-fourths of the states, that won't be an easy process."

"So, we make it easy then."

"And how would we do that, Mr. President?"

"Simple. We put it in the amendment that if the nation is at war, then in order to ensure our national defense and maintain continuity, the president can postpone a presidential election indefinitely.

"Since we will be at war, we can persuade many of the state legislatures to vote to approve the amendment on the grounds of national security. I can just keep us at war forever. They wouldn't want to see our country fall into Democratic leadership and then be overrun by China, would they?"

"Oh, Mr. President, I love the way you think. If only we would have had you in power sooner, we could have prevented so much of our political counterparts' agenda from being enacted."

"Go make it happen, Mitch."

CHAPTER 14

THE PROCLAMATION

"I HOLD IT THAT A LITTLE REBELLION NOW AND THEN IS A GOOD THING, AND AS NECESSARY IN THE POLITICAL WORLD AS STORMS IN THE PHYSICAL. UNSUCCESSFUL REBELLIONS INDEED GENERALLY ESTABLISH THE ENCROACHMENTS ON THE RIGHTS OF THE PEOPLE WHO HAVE PRODUCED THEM. AN OBSERVATION OF THIS TRUTH SHOULD RENDER HONEST REPUBLICAN GOVERNORS SO MILD IN THEIR PUNISHMENT OF REBELLIONS, AS NOT TO DISCOURAGE THEM TOO MUCH. IT IS A MEDICINE NECESSARY FOR THE SOUND HEALTH OF GOVERNMENT."

— THOMAS JEFFERSON

Tuesday, January 5th, 2021

"Good morning once again, Gail Burdock, here with your daily news update. An anonymous source within the White House has revealed to our network that President Vil is threatening to shut down media stations if they continue to report on him in a way that he deems to be negative.

The source claims that the president has grown furious with the negative media coverage. He believes that the media should praise him for his courageous declaration of war against China and that the media is the enemy of the people for not encouraging the people to rally around him and unite in solidarity. Many political pundits are beginning to say the president is becoming increasingly tyrannical."

URGENCY TO IMPLEMENT

January 5th, 2021

Conrad quickly made his way to the governor's new command center in an undisclosed location. He had just received an urgent request to meet with her, but he was not told the details of the meeting request.

"Oh good Conrad, I'm glad you could get here so quickly. We are going to have to move up our timeline for the first phase of our operation," explained Governor Perez.

"How far forward do we need to move things?" Conrad asked.

"It must be tomorrow at 6 p.m., our time."

"That's moving everything forward several weeks. That may be impossible to enact successfully. May I ask why the last-minute urgent change?"

"We've just been informed that Vil is trying to revoke the licenses of broadcast television stations that cover him responsibly by the end of this week. That will take them offline and reduce the reach of my address to the nation that we planned for the night before Vil was to be unconstitutionally sworn in for another term."

"It doesn't surprise me at this point. He is an egomaniac and thrives on positive things being said about him."

"Can you make it happen?"

"We are already capable of disrupting every television and radio transmission. We can also interrupt cable and satellite programming to bring your address to the nation. The only thing we are still working on is the telecommunications network. I can press my telecommunications team to focus all their efforts on ensuring your broadcast will stream live across every cell phone in the nation."

"Good, let them know we need this to work, and we are counting on them. If we are to compel the nation to stand up for our democracy, this is our best chance. We have to reach the widest audience possible, and hope the credibility of governors and me prevail."

"I will get the team to speed things up."

"And what about the other parts of the first phase?"

"You mean the power grid?"

"Yes. Will we be able to shut down the nation's entire power grid and telecommunications networks in time? If this doesn't work as planned, then Vil will be able to use the satellite systems and every asset at his hands to track our movement. This is truly the most pivotal part.

"If we are to have any chance of taking back the country from this authoritarian, then we need to move swiftly and undetected before he can use the military and law enforcement agencies to his advantage. We would like to keep the number of fatalities to a minimum; in fact, it would be ideal to not have any, but I don't see that as a possibility."

"Well, let me get back to my team so we can ensure this works in time."

"Very well, and Conrad, be sure to tell everyone that they are doing great work for the nation and that we will soon restore our democracy."

Conrad left his meeting with the governor and stepped outside to grab some fresh air before returning to his team.

"Is this really going to happen in just a few hours?" he thought to himself. "What if this doesn't go as planned, and the majority of Americans aren't willing to stand up to fight for freedom and democracy? What if this whole thing goes awry and everyone is rounded up will be charged with treason?

"We are already expecting to be outnumbered, and we will be going up against the most powerful military in the world. What happens if we don't convince enough military members to abandon their posts and join our side? There is so much doubt, and so little time left before we test our theory, that good will prevail over evil."

As Conrad gazed hopelessly out onto the mountains in the distance, he began to recall his moments in Afghanistan once more.

Conrad unsnapped his M9 pistol attached at his side. He turned the handle and slowly opened the door, slightly exposing the back end of the MRAP. Outside stood an officer with the Afghan National Police, a liaison to their team that was part of the last vehicle in their convoy. Feeling more secure, knowing he was a trusted member of their team, he opened the door ever more slightly.

That's when it happened. The officer lifted his pistol and aimed directly at Conrad. BANG! BANG! BANG! He was hit three times, thrusting him backward and off his feet. The officer pulled the door completely open, taking aim at the other service members of the team. BANG! BANG! Two shots hit Mustafa Wali, one to his left leg, the other grazed his waist, just below his protective armor.

BANG! BANG! One shot directly hit one of the cryptologists in the head. The other grazed the shoulder of the remaining cryptologist. BANG! BANG! BANG! The officer fell backward and onto the ground. Conrad's heart was racing.

"What had just happened?" he thought.

He leaped outside the MRAP and kicked the officer's gun away. He bent down to check his pulse. He was dead. He jumped back into the MRAP and found Mustafa bleeding uncontrollably from his left leg. The bullet had hit his femoral artery. He yelled at the other cryptologist to check the pulse of the one shot in the head. It was clear from the gunshot wound that he did not make it.

Conrad reached for the first aid kit in the back of the MRAP, grabbing some gauze and applying pressure to the wound to stop the bleeding. Mustafa had lost a lot of blood and would need to be transported back to the base hospital for immediate medical attention, and blood transfusion.

He looked up at Conrad and mumbled for him to check if he had been shot. Conrad didn't feel any pain, he checked his uniform and he didn't see blood anywhere. He realized the officer shot him three times, each time directly hitting his vest. Conrad wondered how the officer had hit his vest and missed his body at such a close range.

BACK TO REALITY

Conrad's heart was now racing as he returned to the present moment. So much had happened during that encounter. Conrad was able to successfully control the bleeding from Mustafa's leg, but he had lost one of his fellow servicemembers. Their SEAL team eventually took out the Taliban members that ambushed them. They gathered their fallen comrades and went back to the base. Their mission was never executed and was over before it began.

They eventually learned that the officer in the Afghan National Police had been threatened by the Taliban. They threatened the life of his family if he did not turn and become a spy for them. When he informed the Taliban of that specific mission, they again threatened his family. This time he had to take out as many members of the team after the Taliban ambushed them.

Conrad had put his days in the armed forces and all of the long deployments in the past. He thought all of that ended when he left the Navy. But now he found himself on the verge of war, a civil war on American soil.

ANOTHER TRAITOR EMERGES

January 6th, 2021

Conrad suddenly awakened from a deep sleep. He had been resting in his bunk, trying to catch just a few hours of rest before everything goes into action.

It was the last time he would sleep in the bunk before they move to a new location for security reasons. Peering around the almost empty room, he noticed a figure near the foot of his bunk.

"Jasmine, what are you doing here?" he asked.

"Conrad, I think we have an emergency to attend to."

"Of course we do," he replied sarcastically, "What is going on now?"

"One of the members of our team has disappeared. We haven't been able to find him anywhere in the building, and no one had seen him since around this time yesterday."

"Are you sure? There are a lot of people operating in this building, maybe we just need to search it again."

"No, Conrad, he is a traitor to the cause. We checked his computer and were able to track communications back to the NSA. We can't track it exactly where inside NSA, but we have tracked the communications with NSA all the way back to December 24th, the same day that he arrived here and joined the team."

"This is what I was afraid of by taking on all these outsiders. We didn't have time to vet them before bringing them in. If he leaked anything, at least he only has one small piece of our operations. What part of the mission was he involved in?"

"He was working on the remote operations team. He may have been privy to the locations of all of our leaders."

"Okay, this is urgent. But, as always, I'm glad you are on our core team and came up with a plan for numerous locations for our leadership teams."

"We've always been a good team together. I sure miss working with you, Conrad. I don't think I could have ever predicted we would be involved in something this historic. The last time we saw each other, I was getting engaged, and you were starting your first year of teaching. The future looked so bright."

"I know, it seemed like the best days were ahead of us. As the cliché goes, 'for every two steps forward, there is one step back.' I guess we took too many steps forward that nature decided to jump in and push us several steps back. But let's not focus on the past; we need to look forward because we have a very uphill battle ahead of us."

"Well, that's something you don't hear from a history teacher often. You are always focused on the past."

Conrad shrugged, "We will have plenty of time at some point to focus on how we got here. For now, we need to implement the backup plan and communicate with all of our leaders so we can get them to relocate to new remote locations."

"On it, we will get them to relocate today."

"They need to relocate now. Everything starts tonight and we can't have them scrambling around once the nation goes dark or it will be too late."

THE LAST AMERICANS

January 6th, 2021

Governor Perez proceeded down the long corridor to the room at the end. It had been converted into a temporary studio for her to address the nation. As she entered the room, she felt the gravity of the moment flush over her. This was not a moment she ever envisioned occurring in her lifetime.

The steady stream of complacency had become all too commonplace for Americans that no one saw this moment coming. A corrupt president that refused to concede an election that he lost had found a way to retain power. The nation, although not formally in a state of declared civil war, was already in a de facto one.

This was her chance to unite the resistance movements and restore the nation before it is too late. She stepped up to the podium, looked into the camera, and awaited the signal from the camera crew that the broadcast was live.

"My fellow Americans, I stand before you tonight not as a governor, but as the leader of a coalition of Americans that have united to remove an unduly elected president and restore our Democratic Republic. We find ourselves living in uncertain times. Four years ago, Donald E. Vil became our president with the assistance of the Russian Federation, which conducted election meddling and interfered in our election process.

"Two months ago, the Russians repeated their election meddling and failed. Mr. Vil then used the power of the presidency to deceive the American people once more by lying to every American about the actions he and the Russians executed by diverting the blame to China.

"I tell you this because we find ourselves at the moment in time where we must recognize that in only a few shorts days, he will no longer be the legitimate President of the United States of America. He has committed treason against this nation, and he must be held to account for his actions. We, the people, must compel him to step down from the office he was not re-elected to hold.

"If he chooses not to relinquish power, then patriotic citizens all across this great nation must stand and bear arms to remove him from power. We, too, must recognize that anyone that bears arms in his defense or provides aid and comfort to him is willing to have arms brought against them.

"We do not want a civil war. But if Mr. Vil does not acknowledge our call for him to step down, and if citizens are willing to stand in defense of his position, then we have no choice but to engage in one. We are a Coalition of Patriots that stand for the principles that gave birth to our nation and were fought for through a civil war once before.

"We are calling on all patriotic Americans to join us so that we can remove Mr. Vil from the office he does not legitimately hold so that we can restore our Democratic Republic and return to peace. There are events that unfold in the course of human history that serve as warning signs for us in the present, to prevent us from repeating the same mistakes as the generations that came before.

"Oftentimes, we ignore those warning signs and instead follow down that eerily familiar path hoping, wanting, and yearning for a different outcome. We frequently do not find that different outcome, and so we look back on our mistakes and promise to never repeat them again. We even document the occasions to serve as a warning sign for a future generation to prevent them from repeating similar events.

"However, this time, we do not have the fortune of standing by and repeating the same mistakes of the generations that preceded us. For if we do, then our nation will be no more; our freedoms will cease to exist; our entire way of life will be lost. We now find ourselves on the precipice of a second Civil War in order to prevent that outcome.

"We have often found our nation in times of war and uncertainty. Great leaders have emerged in those times to give us hope for the future. So let me use the words of the leaders that brought us to hope in some of those times of despair to serve as a reminder, once again, that we will get through this and victory will prevail over the darkness and illegitimacy that stands before us.

"These were the words of Franklin Roosevelt when he spoke to the nation in the darkness of our Second World War, where he quoted two of our founding fathers. Here are his words:

"The task that we Americans now face will test us to the uttermost. Never before have we been called upon for such a prodigious effort. Never before have we had so little time in which to do so much.

"These are the times that try men's souls."

"Tom Paine wrote those words on a drumhead, by the light of a campfire.

"That was when Washington's little army of ragged, rugged men was retreating across New Jersey, having tasted naught but defeat. And General Washington ordered that these great words were written by Tom Paine be read to the men of every regiment in the Continental Army, and this was the assurance given to the first American armed forces:

"The summer soldier and the sunshine patriot will, in this crisis, shrink from the service of their country; but he that stands it now, deserves the love and thanks of man and woman. Tyranny, like hell, is not easily conquered, yet we have this consolation with us, that the harder the sacrifice, the more glorious the triumph.

"So spoke Americans in the year 1776. So speak Americans today!

"Those words I believe ring true at this moment in our history as they did in those times.

"A wise person once told me, 'when democracy dies in America, democracy dies everywhere.' Well, my fellow Americans, we now find ourselves at that very moment where democracy is collapsing all around us. We must make that pivotal choice if we can consider it a choice at all.

"Will we stand to save democracy in America so that it can continue to shine brightly around us and serve as a beacon of hope to the world? Or will we choose to allow for people of ill-intention to continue to erode our democratic way of life, leaving us to perish? We cannot stand by and let this moment in our human history pass us by while we do nothing. For if we are willing to give up our Democracy, to purchase a little temporary security, we deserve neither Democracy nor Security.

"Therefore, your country is calling on you, every freedom and democracy-loving American, to come forward and be willing to fight against the dark shadow of tyranny before us. Your nation needs you now more than ever before, and if, at this moment, we choose to step forward, our nation shall not perish from the earth. America needs every one of us."

The camera shut off, the overhead lights went dim, and the camera crew signaled that the live video feed had been shut off. She stepped back from the podium and walked over to the small contingent at the far end of the room as they waited to escort her to another secure location. It was beginning; the nation was now at war.

Conrad looked over to the governor for her signal so that he could implement the start of the second phase. When they locked eyes from across the room, she gave the nod of her head to acknowledge him and allow him to proceed. Conrad turned and looked down the long corridor and gave his team the signal to commence.

Then came, the rolling noise of the telecommunications towers and power grids shutting down all over the country, as everything came to a grinding halt and the nation went dark.

www.ingramcontent.com/pod-product-compliance
Lightning Source LLC
Chambersburg PA
CBHW030744110726
47900CB00008B/2452

9780578671659